SELECTED CHANSONS

RECENT RESEARCHES IN THE MUSIC OF THE RENAISSANCE

James Haar, general editor

A-R Editions, Inc., publishes six quarterly series—

Recent Researches in the Music of the Middle Ages and Early Renaissance
Margaret Bent, general editor

Recent Researches in the Music of the Renaissance
James Haar, general editor

Recent Researches in the Music of the Baroque Era
Robert L. Marshall, general editor

Recent Researches in the Music of the Classical Era
Eugene K. Wolf, general editor

Recent Researches in the Music of the Nineteenth and Early Twentieth Centuries
Rufus Hallmark, general editor

Recent Researches in American Music
H. Wiley Hitchcock, general editor—

which make public music that is being brought to light
in the course of current musicological research.

Each volume in the *Recent Researches* is devoted
to works by a single composer or to a single genre of composition,
chosen because of its potential interest to scholars and performers,
and prepared for publication according to the standards that govern
the making of all reliable historical editions.

Subscribers to this series, as well as patrons of subscribing institutions,
are invited to apply for information about the "Copyright-Sharing Policy"
of A-R Editions, Inc., under which the contents of this volume
may be reproduced free of charge for study or performance.

Correspondence should be addressed:

A-R EDITIONS, INC.
315 West Gorham Street
Madison, Wisconsin 53703

RECENT RESEARCHES IN THE MUSIC OF THE RENAISSANCE • VOLUME LXVIII

SELECTED CHANSONS

from British Library, MS Additional 35087

Edited by William M. McMurtry
Texts Established and Translated
by Arthur J. Gionet

A-R EDITIONS, INC. • MADISON

Library of Congress Cataloging in Publication Data
Main entry under title:

Selected chansons from British Library, ms. Additional
    35087.

    (Recent researches in the music of the Renaissance,
ISSN 0486–123X ; v. 68)
    For 3–4 voices.
    "The performance medium should be vocal throughout
with one voice to a part"—Pref.
    French words, also printed as texts with English
translations following each chanson.
    Includes bibliographical references.
    1. Chansons, Polyphonic.   2. Vocal trios,
Unaccompanied.   3. Vocal quartets, Unaccompanied.
I. McMurtry, William M.   II. British Library.
Manuscript. Additional 35087.   III. Series.
M2.R2384   vol. 68   [M1529.4]   84–760433
ISBN 0–89579–148–X (pbk.)

Contents

Preface

The Manuscript and Its Owners

Chanson literature of the late fifteenth and early sixteenth centuries, with its intermingling of courtly and popular elements, represents a pinnacle in secular music of the middle Renaissance and provides songs and texts that are delightful to study and perform. The British Library, Manuscript Additional 35087, hereafter referred to as London Add. 35087, is a major source of this repertory from which one four-voice[1] and twenty-three three-voice chansons have been selected for this edition. These pieces were chosen for the following reasons. First, they include all of the French secular music that is unique to this chansonnier or that is hitherto unpublished in major modern anthologies. Second, they exemplify the major three- and four-voice chanson styles of the turn of the sixteenth century and mark the significant transition from the imitative style of Josquin Desprez's generation to the homophonic–lightly polyphonic style of the early sixteenth century. Third, the chordal-polyphonic works antedate the Parisian chanson of the second quarter of the sixteenth century by nearly two decades and demonstrate the importance of the manuscript as an early source for pieces in the Parisian style. The four-voice composition is no. 5, and the *unica* are nos. 1, 3, 5, 8, 9, 12, 13, 14, 15, 17, 18, 20, 21, and 22 of the edition. Composers of the pieces in the edition include Benedictus Appenzeller, Josquin Desprez, Antoine de Févin, Johannes Ghiselin [Verbonnet], Jean Mouton, Ninot le Petit, and Jo. de Vyzeto.

London Add. 35087 is a large octavo parchment manuscript of ninety-five folios that contains thirty-six French chansons, twenty-five Flemish chansons, fourteen Latin motets, two works with Italian texts, and one motet-chanson, all arranged in choirbook format (see Plate I).[2] (See, also, Appendix B: Contents of London Add. 35087.) Most manuscripts from the turn of the sixteenth century were costly items of luxury, and their contents reflect the wide-ranging tastes of the members of the aristocracy and wealthy bourgeoisie who could afford them. London Add. 35087 is no exception. Although it lacks the beautiful decorations and illuminations of some contemporary sources, the chansonnier contains elaborate initials and careful writing of both music and texts, with few omissions of notes or words.

According to the Latin inscription on the opening folio ("Hieronymus Laurinus est meus herus," meaning "Jérôme Lauweryn is my master"), Jérôme Lauweryn (Lauwerin, Laurin), a wealthy Flemish nobleman, commissioned the manuscript. Lauweryn, lord of Watervliet and Poortvliet, served in the governments of three regents of the Burgundian Netherlands: Maximilian, Hapsburg archduke of Austria, later to become Holy Roman Emperor; his son, Philip the Handsome, also archduke of Austria and, later, king of Castile; and his daughter, Marguerite of Austria, widow of both the heir to the Spanish throne and the duke of Savoy. As general receiver (mayor) of the Franc, or castellany, of Bruges (the rural area surrounding the city of Bruges from Dixmunde to Eekloo and Biervliet) from 1487 until 1498, and as counselor, chamberlain, and treasurer general of the finances under Philip the Handsome from 1497 on, Jérôme guided the collecting of taxes and other revenues from the province of Flanders.[3] Having acquired favor and wealth in discharging his duties, he directed his energy and money into reclaiming land from the sea in northern Flanders between the present towns of Boekhoute and St.-Jan-in-Eremo.[4] Between 1501 and 1506, Jérôme established the Kristoffelpolder, Jeroompolder, Philipspolder, Maria, Barbara, and Hellepolders, and other polder land in this vicinity of the Scheldt River.[5] Philip the Handsome responded by awarding his treasurer the fiefs of Watervliet, Waterdizk, and Waterland on this reclaimed land. In 1504, Lauweryn founded and enclosed the town of Watervliet in the Kristoffelpolder and built its church and cloth mill; in 1506, he built the town of Philippine in the Philipspolder, named in honor of his generous patron.[6] In recounting Philip the Handsome's second voyage to Spain and subsequent death, an anonymous chronicler attacked Jérôme for mismanaging and embezzling his regent's finances.[7] However, no other documentation supports this accusation, and accounts indicate that he continued to hold his high office in the new regency of Marguerite of Austria until he was forced to retire in 1508 because of ill health.[8] In 1507, Maximilian purchased Jérôme's home in Malines for Marguerite, and it served as her residence and seat of government for the remainder of her life.[9] Jérôme died in 1509,[10] and his death establishes the terminating point for London Add. 35087 since the majority of the compositions were probably copied at one time by one group of scribes (with the exception of the last two pieces in the manuscript, listed as nos. 77 and 78 in Appendix B, which were recorded by later, inferior scribes). Undoubtedly, Jérôme was a man of learning and a connoisseur of the arts. The excellence of the court chapel under Philip the Handsome, which included Pierre de la Rue, Antoine Divitis, Mabriano de Orto, and Alexander Agricola, among others,[11] may have stimulated his appreciation of music, and the sizable number of Flemish pieces interspersed throughout the manuscript may represent his predilection for chansons in his native tongue.

In bequeathing his fortune and position to his sons, Jérôme supplied his heirs with the means to devote themselves to learning and humanistic pursuits. His sons Matthias (died 1540), Mark (1488–1540), Peter (1489–ca. 1522), Charles (1506–52), and James (died 1512) were all acquaintances of Erasmus of Rotterdam. Matthias, the eldest, succeeded to his father's estates and in turn fathered two great antiquaries, Mark and Guy.[12] Guy, the younger, was born in Bruges in 1532 and died in Lille in 1589. Trained in law, he set up practice in Bruges in 1557 and became his brother's collaborator in numismatic endeavors. Mark, who was born at Bruges in 1530 and died in Calais in 1581, succeeded his father, Matthias, as lord of Watervliet and Waterland and receiver of the Franc of Bruges. Over the years, his wealth allowed him to assemble an impressive collection of rare books, precious manuscripts, medals, and coins, which he kept in his country house outside Bruges. These treasures, which probably included Jérôme's chansonnier, now London Add. 35087, were admired by erudite men everywhere.[13] During the religious disturbances of 1578, Bruges was captured by the army of the Scottish colonel Henry Balfour. During his attempt to escape to Ostend, Mark was robbed of the collection of coins and precious documents which he had carried with him. Meanwhile, his mansion and country house at Bruges were ransacked during his absence and many other items were taken. What remained of his treasures was further dispersed at his death, since he died unmarried. Some of the stolen documents and coins were discovered later in England, and it is conceivable that London Add. 35087 was transported across the English Channel by a soldier and sold as well.[14] An inscription on folio 75, verso, of the manuscript, which reads, "There ys little such p[ar]chment now to be had any where for money," and another on folio 37, verso, which reads, "Com all Tru Harted Lovers and Har," appear to be in sixteenth-century hands. However, there is no evidence of an English owner of the manuscript until Herbert Thompson presented it to the British Library in 1897.

Music and Texts

The French repertory of London Add. 35087 comprises a variety of text forms and compositional styles that were current at the turn of the sixteenth century. Like many chansonniers from this period, the manuscript contains both courtly and popular pieces, as well as works in which the courtly and popular types coalesce. Nine chansons musicales illustrate the courtly type, some of the twenty-seven chansons rustiques exemplify the popular category, and other chansons rustiques represent the type in which the courtly tradition has been transformed by the introduction of popular elements. From this repertory, twenty-four strophic pieces and chansons with refrains (chansons à refrains), including fourteen unica, have been selected for this edition. Each of these chansons is identified as a musicale or a rustique in the Critical Commentary section.

Chansons musicales

The learned chansons musicales mark the continuing, though diminishing, interest in refined polyphonic songs among nobles and aristocrats of the Renaissance courts. To a large extent, the sophisticated texts of these pieces reflect the medieval courtly themes of unrequited love, inconsolable grief, and melancholy. They follow either the rondeau form, the most important of the medieval fixed forms (formes fixes) still employed around 1500, or new free chanson forms, which contain varying stanza lengths and rhyme schemes and text repetitions; if refrains appear in alternation with the strophes in these free forms, they are not rigidly prescribed as with the rondeau.

The musical styles associated with the chansons musicales mirror the changes in secular musical composition of the time. First, the Franco-Netherlandish chanson style of the late fifteenth century is employed in London Add. 35087 rondeaux by Hayne van Ghizeghem and Alexander Agricola (nos. 26 and 35 of Appendix B) and an anonymous composer (no. 67 of Appendix B). A dominant superius coupled to a supporting tenor, an independent contratenor, and melismatic phrases of varying lengths are among the features of this style. Second, a modified Franco-Netherlandish style incorporating more clear-cut phrases, some imitation, and a less melismatic approach to text settings is used in two other rondeaux from London Add. 35087 by Loyset Compère (nos. 27 and 61 of Appendix B). (Since the chansons representing these styles already appear in modern editions, they are not included here.) Third, the equal voice style of imitative counterpoint developed in the works of Josquin Desprez at the end of the fifteenth century is utilized in four free chansons musicales from the manuscript. These are included in the edition as nos. 2, 4, 7, and 24. Systematic imitation among voices, short homorhythmic sections, phrase repetitions, and more syllabic text settings are features of these pieces.

Chansons musicales of the late fifteenth and early sixteenth centuries are often based on pre-existing cantus prius facti. Unlike the contemporary chansons rustiques, however, the borrowed material in chansons musicales is taken from polyphonic rather than monophonic sources. For example, an anonymous London Add. 35087 *rondeau* (no. 67 of Appendix B) is one of over thirty settings of *Fors seulement* melodies linked to an original three-voice arrangement by Johannes Ockeghem.[15] On the other hand, all of the free *chansons musiclaes* of the edition may represent the original arrangements of their melodies. Numbers 2, 4, and 24 have no concordances to prove or disprove this hypothesis, but no. 7 appears to be the first setting of its tenor *cantus prius factus,* providing the basis for two other, later arrangements (see Critical Commentary).

Chansons rustiques

In contrast, the texts of the *chansons rustiques* deal with the middle class social milieu, and the pieces provided entertainment for drinking, festival occasions, dancing, and the French secular theater.[16] The much larger number of popular chansons in London Add. 35087 reflects the increasing interest in the real world of urban and common people. Unlike those of the *chanson musicale,* the texts of the popular chansons are much more wide-ranging and varied. The wit, verve, and satire of everyday life replace the elegance and idealized emotions of the court. While love is the principal theme of the *chanson musicale,* it is just one of many subjects for the popular chansons; when it is treated in the *chansons rustiques,* it is often dealt with satirically or in a naive or bucolic manner.[17] The *chanson rustique* poems are usually strophic, with a wide variety of stanza arrangements and rhyme schemes, some resembling the old *virelai* and *ballade.* A preference for assonance rather than rhyme is another identifiable feature, and refrains punctuate the strophic structure of a few poems, creating the *chanson à refrain.* In their variety of construction, these *chansons à refrains* contrast noticeably with the conventional *rondeau* form of the *chanson musicale.*

The *chansons rustiques* appear to be derived from pre-existing monophonic music. Popular monophony was widely performed in the fifteenth and early sixteenth centuries, but sources for this repertory are few. Two monophonic chansonniers from the beginning of the sixteenth century, Paris, Bibliothèque Nationale, MS fonds fr. 9346 and MS fonds fr. 12744, have survived and contain the melodies of nine *chansons rustiques* from London Add. 35087. Four of these nine chansons appear in other modern editions and so are excluded from this anthology (nos. 12, 52, 70, and 77 of Appendix B). The other five pieces are included in this edition (nos. 3, 6, 12, 16, and 23). Similarities in melodic shape, phrase length, and text underlay between the tenors of the popular chansons and their models attest to their pre-existing monophonic state. As Howard Brown explains, these "melodies are simple and straightforward; the ranges are narrow, the phrase structure regular, and the rhythm uncomplicated."[18]

They mirror the shape of the words, and melodic repetitions often reflect the rhyme schemes and verse repetitions of the poetry. Since all other *chansons rustiques* from London Add. 35087 contain similar melodic and textual characteristics, they must also be based on monophonic models, even though these models remain unknown.

The *chanson rustique* melodies are set in several compositional styles of which three are represented in the manuscript and edition.[19] The first is the Josquin style of imitative counterpoint found initially in sources dating from between ca. 1470 and 1500 and later in manuscripts associated with the court of France during the reign of Louis XII (1498–1515). In this style, the simple borrowed melody is placed in the tenor and imitated by the newly composed superius and contratenor. All three voices are similar in their melodic and rhythmic features and are equal in range; but the tenor can be distinguished as the *cantus prius factus.* The tenor preserves the repetition scheme, and since it is the simplest statement of the melody, it must be acknowledged as the pre-existing form of the tune.[20] The polyphonic texture is worked out systematically, with both imitative and freely contrapuntal continuations extending the length of the music for the outer voices to bring cadences in all parts together. Attention is given to proper text accentuation, and often short homorhythmic patterns of minims are interspersed into the polyphonic framework to which the texts are underlaid syllabically.

Fifteen *chansons rustiques,* the largest number of popular chansons from London Add. 35087, are composed in this first style. Four of these, two pieces by Josquin Desprez (nos. 8 and 12 of Appendix B) and one each by Antoine Brumel and Antoine de Févin (nos. 70 and 77 of Appendix B), already appear in modern editions and so are not included here. The eleven others, all in this edition, consist of two by Antoine de Févin (nos. 8 and 19), one each by Jean Mouton and Josquin Desprez (nos. 6 and 16), and seven anonymous pieces (nos. 1, 10, 13, 14, 18, 20, and 21).

This repertory appears to have been appreciated at the court of Louis XII of France, where, in the first and second decades of the sixteenth century, the nobles developed a novel taste for popular songs and texts. Josquin, Févin, and Mouton were all prominent composers connected to the French court at this time, and their chansons are also contained in other manuscripts associated with Louis XII's reign: Paris, Bibliothèque Nationale, MS fonds fr. 9346, prepared for one of the king's great nobles, Charles de Bourbon, and the monophonic source for some of our *chansons rustiques;* and Cambridge, Magdalene College, MS Pepys 1760, a major source of Févin chansons. Brown suggests that this courtly predilection for songs about the middle and lower classes is a reflection of the drawing together of the different classes of French society into a closer relationship and helped to initiate the reconciliation of courtly and popular elements in the later sixteenth-century chanson.[21]

The second compositional style, in which the borrowed material is stated by the upper voices in a two-part canon accompanied by two other free voices, emerged in the first quarter of the sixteenth century. London Add. 35087 contains only two such works, one, by Mouton, which is not included in the edition (no. 52 of Appendix B), and one, a *unicum* by Jo. de Vyzeto, which is included in the edition as no. 5.

The third compositional style also dates from the first quarter of the sixteenth century and exhibits a homophonic and lightly polyphonic framework in which the *cantus prius factus* appears either in the tenor or superius, with both voices often moving in parallel sixths. Phrases are short and well defined, voice ranges are narrow, texts are usually strophic and set syllabically, and overall lengths of works are short. The simplicity of this style contrasts conspicuously with the contrapuntal sophistication of the preceding styles. Ten *chansons rustiques* from the source follow the third style. One piece by Févin (no. 49 of Appendix B) and an anonymous work (no. 41 of Appendix B) are not in this edition, but the eight others are included here: individual chansons by Benedictus Appenzeller (no. 3), Jean Mouton (no. 11), and Johannes Ghiselin [Verbonnet] (no. 12) and five anonymous pieces (nos. 9, 15, 17, 22, and 23). These chansons appear to derive their melodies from the same pre-existing monophonic literature and show the same keen interest in popular culture enjoyed at the court of Louis XII as do the works of the first style. However, the fact that ten pieces from the manuscript are in the third style may point to a significant shift from the imitative to the chordal–lightly polyphonic style in the course of the first twenty years of the sixteenth century.

According to Brown, these homophonic works anticipate the development of the chordal Parisian chanson as composed by Claudin de Sermisy in the late 1520s and 1530s.[22] Pieces by Claudin, a major composer at the court of Francis I, and his text collaborator, Clément Marot, closely resemble the musical structure and poetic form and content of the pieces in the third style with a few differences. Claudin primarily wrote four-voice rather than three-voice arrangements;[23] he did not borrow pre-existing monophonic material as the serious composers of Louis XII's court did but composed his own melodies based on the popular *cantus prius facti*. Finally, Claudin's tunes are placed in the superius rather than in the tenor, while it can be argued that the melody of a chanson in the third style is stated either in the tenor or superius or both at the same time. Similarly, the simple and direct language of the *chansons rustiques* affected the development of the vibrant and sometimes obscene texts of Marot. Brown theorizes that if a newly composed chanson by a court composer (e.g., Claudin) is set to a text by a

poet close to the court (e.g., Marot) and is included in a collection containing *chansons musicales* (e.g., an anthology of Pierre Attaingnant), then the piece must be considered a *chanson musicale*.[24] But Claudin's courtly chansons contain musical and textual features of the popular chanson and even look like *chansons rustiques*. Therefore, it seems that his pieces portray the complete coalescence of the courtly and popular elements, and the homorhythmic *chansons rustiques* of the edition anticipate this reconciliation of *musicale* and *rustique* types.

The Chansons of This Edition

As mentioned before, the melancholic and unrequited aspects of love cloud the poetry of the four *chansons musicales* in the edition. Ninot le Petit's *chanson débat* (one of several genres of the traditional courtly love songs which gives each lover a turn at expressing a solution to a problem of love), no. 4, is a lovers' argument concerning which lover is more miserable than the other; lines 1, 3, and 5 are spoken by the woman, while lines 2 and 4 are expressed by the man. A man's discouragement and sorrow in loving a woman color the poem of Appenzeller's *Tout plain d'ennuy*, no. 24. An anonymous work, no. 7, projects the traditional view of male service and sacrifice for a lady. In another anonymous piece, no. 2, the "friend"-lover speaks to himself before urging his lady to love him.

Sources among the concordances attribute Ninot le Petit's chanson, no. 4, to Adrian Willaert and Clément Janequin, also. According to François Lesure, however, the attributions to Janequin have been discredited.[25] Willaert is, of course, a major representative of a later generation of composers, and I believe that the ascription to him is erroneous in light of his youth (born ca. 1490) at the time of the compilation of London Add. 35087. Moreover, no. 4 can be considered representative of what is known about Ninot's style. Number 2 is an anonymous piece whose *secunda pars* is supplied here from a concordance (Uppsala, Universitetsbiblioteket, Vokalmusik i handskrift, MS 76a) in order to provide as full and complete a setting of the chanson as possible. There is no composer-attribution in any source for no. 7, and all concordances for no. 24 attribute that work to Appenzeller.

In the *chansons rustiques* love is handled more directly and satirically. Many of their texts reflect the female side of love and marriage and are expressed by women. These include, in no. 16, the complaints of the *mal mariée* (the young wife married to an old man who is cuckolded), with a response from the lady's lover, and, in no. 23, a statement from an advocate of the cuckold's viewpoint. One poem is a woman's obscene lament of her husband's crudity, no. 11. Other texts bemoan the restrictions of marriage, no. 10, and having children, no. 13. In no. 12, an unmarried lady's avowal of love is answered by her lover's response, and in no. 3, three women enjoy themselves in a lively drinking song not related to love at all. Other texts directed to women but expressed by men include lovers' pleas, no. 9 (a dance song which definitely combines the affected grief and anguish of the courtly chanson with the earthy imagery of the *chanson rustique*) and no. 15; no. 19, a pastoral song associating the man's love for his "little snub nose" with Robin and Marion, the traditional shepherd and shepherdess; and no. 22, an earthy tribute to woman's physical endowments. In addition, one poem, no. 20, treats the anticipated pleasures of love as expressed by either a man or a woman. Stanzas (with or without refrains) vary in length from three lines (nos. 10 and 15) to eight lines (nos. 1, 5, 6, and 9) and show an assortment of rhyme schemes. Verse lines range in length from six syllables to thirteen syllables, with a majority consisting of eight syllables. It is not uncommon to find short lines mixed with longer lines in some of the poems also. The three *chansons à refrains* among the *chansons rustiques* show a variety of arrangements as well: no. 3 gives a single-line opening and closing refrain for each stanza; no. 16 has a three-line refrain following the first stanza; and no. 19 places a two-line opening and closing refrain around its three-line stanza.

Of the many *chansons rustiques* written in the first style of imitative counterpoint, Josquin's *chanson à refrain*, no. 16, Févin's *chanson à refrain*, no. 19, and Mouton's strophic piece, no. 6, employ the paraphrase technique in which the superius, tenor, and contratenor share in the statement of the borrowed melody.[26] In these pieces, phrase motives enter in close imitation in all voices and are extended by continuations directing the flow of the counterpoint toward strongly tonal common cadences. However, the middle section of Mouton's work is treated homorhythmically in triple meter. This combination of imitative and homophonic sections and the use of a tenor-contratenor duo without superius at the end of the first section mark this chanson as unique in the anthology. Févin's work is also attributed to Josquin in Le Roy and Ballard, RISM 1578[15], but this ascription must be refuted on stylistic grounds.[27]

Jo. de Vyzeto's chanson, no. 5, the sole canonic piece in the second style included in the edition, is based possibly on a German folksong. The realization of the canonic voice above the superius results in the only four-voice setting here.

The homophonic pieces of the third compositional style that most closely parallel the later Parisian chanson are Mouton's complaint concerning male crudity, no. 11, and three anonymous works, nos. 9, 15, and 23.[28] In addition to the homorhythmic movement with the *cantus prius factus* often in the superius, phrase repetition, syllabic text underlay, brevity, and such other devices as three-minim anacruses on the same pitches

(nos. 9 and 23) and the I–VI–V chord progression (no. 11) anticipate the features and tonal design of Claudin de Sermisy's pieces. However, another group of pieces in the third style does not adhere to the homophonic structure strictly but adds light counterpoint and greater rhythmic diversity among voices. Appenzeller's drinking song (no. 3), which may carry the earliest known attribution to its composer, shows the borrowed melody in the tenor within a tenor-contratenor duo that supports a more embellished superius. Verbonnet's strophic chanson (no. 12) presents the unadorned borrowed tenor in a homorhythmic framework which also includes parallelism and imitation between the rhythmically active outer voices. Two *unica* show similar characteristics: no. 17 combines homophony with imitative phrase beginnings and nonimitative continuations, whereas no. 22 exhibits a tighter homophonic structure with some rhythmic variety.

As has been shown, London Add. 35087 contains an interesting variety of French music of the middle Renaissance. Its repertory ranges from the older Franco-Netherlandish *chanson musicale* of the late fifteenth century to the three- and four-voice *chanson rustique* arrangements of the early sixteenth century. The large number of *chansons rustiques* in the manuscript and this edition demonstrates the increasing importance of polyphonic settings of pre-existing popular melodies and the shift in emphasis from the imitative to the homophonic–lightly polyphonic style current at the court of France in the first two decades of the sixteenth century. Concomitantly, the large proportion of these pieces indicates a growing taste among nobles and aristocrats for the everyday world of the lower classes and the breakdown of the old dichotomy between the courtly and popular types. But the special significance of London Add. 35087 lies in the fact that its homophonic *chansons rustiques* of the third style precede by nearly twenty years the development of the Parisian chanson and its coalescence of *musicale* and *rustique* features.

Editorial Methods

The selected French chansons of this anthology appear in alphabetical order. Each work is editorially numbered and employs the first line of text for its title. The incipit of each voice contains the original clef, key signature, time signature, and the initial note, excluding preliminary rests. Ranges for the voices of each piece are supplied, and modern clefs, G or G-8 for superius, G-8 for tenor, and G-8 or F for contratenor, are substituted for the original C and F clefs. Only no. 16 contains a G clef in the source. Apart from labeling the tenor in nos. 6 and 13, designations for the voice parts are not provided in the manuscript. Although no voice-part designations appear in the transcriptions, the lines, reading from top to bottom, are understood as superius, tenor, and contratenor.

Note values are halved (except in no. 14), barlines supplied, and (except in no. 9; see below) the modern equivalent used to replace the original *tempus imperfectum diminutum* (₵) meter signature. In no. 14, where there is no reduction in the transcription, the modern $\frac{2}{1}$ meter signature has been substituted for the original *tempus imperfectum* (C) of its first section (mm. 1–16 of the transcription). The following section (mm. 17–23) employs the original *proportio sesquialtera* (₵3), which has been transcribed as $\frac{3}{2}$; the equation ○=♩. has been placed above the staff in measure 17 to denote the proportion between $\frac{2}{1}$ and $\frac{3}{2}$. Number 6 also uses triple meter in the source (at what is m. 35 of the transcription of this work); all voices shift from ₵ to 3, which is transcribed as $\frac{3}{2}$. The equation ♩=♩. given above the staff at this point marks the proportion change from $\frac{2}{2}$ to $\frac{3}{2}$ and is followed by the reverse equation ♩.=♩ placed above the staff in measure 43 to indicate the return of $\frac{2}{2}$ (₵). Although no. 9 is notated with ₵ signs, it has been barred in $\frac{3}{2}$ meter in the transcription because the music of this dance song seems to move in triple meter; however, cadences in measures 5 and 14 are barred in $\frac{2}{2}$ meter. In addition, meter signs of $\frac{3}{2}$ have been inserted at the penultimate measures in the transcriptions of nos. 15 and 22 to elongate the cadential pattern and allow the final note in each voice to fill a complete measure. Another insertion of the $\frac{3}{2}$ meter sign is needed in no. 3 prior to an interior cadence (m. 20 of the transcription). Finally, one other change in meter signature is required in no. 11: at the cadence of the repeated first section in measure 8, a $\frac{1}{2}$ signature has been inserted to accommodate the final note, which appears as a semibreve (◇) rather than a breve (▯) in each voice in the source.

Ligatures in the manuscript are indicated in the transcriptions by solid horizontal brackets placed above the notes concerned. Coloration is shown by broken horizontal brackets encompassing the notes in question, and instances of ligatures and coloration combined are represented by solid brackets set with broken brackets. The most common coloration is *minor color*, the blackening of semibreve and minim ◆ ♩ used interchangeably with ♦ ♪. Coronas (i.e., fermatas) and repeat signs are placed in the transcriptions as found in the manuscript. Although the source gives only a few coronas over breves and longas in internal and final cadences, fermatas appear in all transcriptions to denote the increased value of final longas (transcribed as whole-notes). *Signa congruentiae* provide points of reference in several chansons. In the source *signa* appear in some voices and not in others. Moreover, existent *signa* are often found out of position within the staves and above or below rests or spaces before the notes to which they are linked. Since

there is no reason for the rather free placement of many of these symbols, the edition places them consistently above the notes to which they correspond. In no. 5, a *signum* marks the entry of the canonic voice, producing the only four-voice setting included in the edition. Other *signa* appearing in nos. 1, 9, 12, 15, 19, and 23 indicate the repetition of the initial A or A' section or *cantus prius factus*. Additional *signa* in m. 12 of no. 23 denote the beginning of the last phrase, which is repeated in a variant reading from the only concordant source, London, British Library, MS Harley 5242. Similarly, *signa* in no. 11 (mm. 5 and 17) mark identical phrases at the ends of two sections of the work, which are repeated in variant readings from St. Gall, Stiftsbibliothek, Cod. 462 (Heer Liederbuch), thus indicating that *signa* were also used as repeat signs in manuscripts of the time. One further use of *signa* occurs in no. 17 where the signs mark a medial cadence (m. 10 of the transcription). The editor has not added any *signa* in this transcription.

All key signatures and accidentals (B-flats and E-flats) are placed in the edition as they appear in the manuscript. Two pieces, nos. 5 and 21, contain partial signatures. Number 5 lacks the flat in the signature of its contratenor, and the only B in this voice (m. 25) has an accidental. Number 21 has no flats in the signatures of its voices, but the contratenor shows an accidental before its first B and flat signs at the beginnings of three succeeding staves in the source, where Bs occur; the final source staff of the contratenor excludes the flat sign, probably because no B is present among its notes. As the result of these B-flats, apparent cross-relations occur between the contratenor and superius at what are measures 14, 20, and 33 of the transcription. These have been corrected in the transcription by adding editorial B-flats above the superius in these measures. Editorial accidentals used to apply *musica ficta* are inserted above the notes concerned in the edition. Sharps are supplied to raise the leading tone at cadences, and flats are added to correct cross-relations, to avoid tritones, and to ensure A–B-flat–A, C–B-flat–A, D–E-flat–D, and F–E-flat–D progressions (to preserve the needed half-step in the hexachords).

As in most manuscripts and prints of the early sixteenth century, words are not set accurately under the notes. The editor has attempted to offer practical solutions to problems of text underlay. All voices in all pieces of this edition contain one stanza of text in London Add. 35087, except for no. 21, which has only two lines of an incomplete stanza in all parts, no. 13, which has incomplete stanzas in tenor and contratenor, and the *secunda pars* of no. 2, which has text only in the superius. The edition has text only in the superius for this *secunda pars*, also. For no. 21, both the source and this edition provide text only for the first seventeen measures of the transcription, and for no. 13, a complete underlay for the edition has been prepared by taking the text from the superius part of the source for the other two voices. The single text stanzas underlaid in all other chansons here represent a composite text established editorially from the three readings of text (one from each voice) in each piece in the source. Although the source gives only the first stanza of any given poem, all stanzas and their translations appear after each piece in the edition. Manuscripts and printed collections that are the sources for the additional stanzas presented in the edition are cited in the Critical Commentary. Text variants among the voices in the source and discrepancies between London Add. 35087 and the other sources are recorded in the commentary to the text for each piece. Where sources provide dissimilar added stanzas, variants among them are also reported. Methods for the citation of variants are discussed in the introduction to the Critical Commentary.

Word usage and Old French words or spellings are explained in the commentary to the texts. Many of the old spellings actually denote the pronunciation used in the late fifteenth and early sixteenth centuries. Examples of actual pronunciation, like *ches* for *ces*, are explained in Margery Anthea Baird, ed., *Pierre de Manchicourt: Twenty-Nine Chansons*.[29] If a word or expression is not discussed in the commentary, the reader may assume that it will be found in a standard French dictionary, such as *Harrap's New Standard French and English Dictionary*,[30] provided allowance is made for obvious Old French spellings: *ung* for *un*, *moy* for *moi*, *aultre* for *autre*, *estez* for *etes*, etc.

The following orthographical changes have been made in the texts to avoid confusion: "v" replaces "u" when modern French has made the change (*deuant* becomes *devant*; *souuent* becomes *souvent*); "j" substitutes for "i" (*ie* becomes *je*); the "y" replaces the pronoun "i." The diacritical marks used are limited to the acute accent to identify the past particple (e.g., *aimée*), to the grave accent to distinguish the preposition *à* from the verb *a*, to the cedilla to identify the pronunciation in such words as *sçay* and *sçavez*, and to the diaresis, which is used to indicate that the word has two syllables instead of one as in *ouïr*. Quotation marks are inserted in passages of dialogue and reported speech. Punctuation and capitalization are editorial. Abbreviations have been resolved and expanded, particularly as regards the insertion of the letter "n" in *mon*, *quant*, and *gentilhome* and as regards the words *que*, *qu'il*, *plus*, and *pour*. With the exception of a few chansons where insufficient music prevents the underlaying of word repetitions, all texts given in the source manuscript appear in the transcriptions. In most instances, the music calls for text repetitions not found in the source; these insertions, as well as missing texts supplied from other manuscripts and printed collections, are enclosed in brackets. The translations correspond closely to the ideas expressed in the texts; however, they are not intended to convey the meter or the rhymes of the originals.

Square brackets are used to enclose all editorially added material, except for that already mentioned in this Editorial Methods section or cited in the Critical Commentary.

Notes on Performance

Since (except for the *secunda pars* of no. 2) all voices of the chansons are underlaid with texts, the performance medium should be vocal throughout, with one voice to a part. Male and female voices should be chosen to fit the range and tessitura of each part. Vibrato is appropriate, and the untexted parts of nos. 2 and 21 can be wordlessly vocalized. Like the repertory of other fully texted early sixteenth-century manuscripts (e.g., Cambridge, Magdalene College, MS Pepys 1760, and London, British Library, MS Harley 5242), the London Add. 35087 pieces of the edition mirror local preferences for the new homogeneous vocal sonority of Josquin's time.[31] Other performance options are possible but less desirable: the playing of all voices on soft instruments (flute or recorder, harp, and lute) or loud instruments (shawms and trombone or sackbut) for outdoor occasions, and combined vocal and instrumental performance with one soft instrument doubling each voice.

Acknowledgments

I am indebted to the British Library, London, for allowing me to use MS Add. 35087 for this edition. I wish to express my sincere thanks to Professor Arthur J. Gionet, North Texas State University, for his careful editing and translating of the texts, and Professor Howard M. Brown, who, as general editor of the Recent Researches in the Music of the Renaissance series, read the manuscript and musical transcriptions and offered many helpful suggestions during the preparation of this anthology; his advice on the text underlaying was especially appreciated. For assistance in providing material for concordances, I am grateful to the following libraries: North Texas State University, University of Illinois at Urbana, University of Texas at Austin, and Wichita State University. I further appreciate the efforts of Mr. Terry Basford and the interlibrary loan staff at Oklahoma State University and the directors of the Archives du Nord, Lille, France; Archives Générales du Royaume, Brussels, Belgium; and Centrale Bibliotheek, Rijksuniversiteit, Ghent, Belgium, for supplying other research data. Finally, I thank Professor Arthur Wolff for the use of his microfilm collection of manuscripts and prints and my wife for her encouragement and assistance in this project.

William M. McMurtry

Notes

1. This piece becomes a four-voice setting with the realization of a canonic voice.

2. See William M. McMurtry, "The British Museum Manuscript Additional 35087: A Transcription of the French, Italian, and Latin Compositions with Concordance and Commentary" (Ph.D. diss., North Texas State University, 1967), and Johannes Wolf, *25 driestemmige Oud-Nederlandsche Liederen uit het Einde der viftiende Eeuw naar den Codex London British Museum Additional MSS. 35087* (Amsterdam, 1910), for studies and transcriptions of these works.

3. Henry de Vocht, *History of the Foundation and the Rise of the Collegium Trilingue Louvaniense, 1517–1550* (Louvain, 1951–55), 2:67–68; Documents B6774, B6775, and B6776, Archives du Nord, Lille, France; Documents 1246, 1247, 16104, and 7218–20, Chambre des Comptes, Archives Générales du Royaume, Brussels, Belgium.

4. L. Roersch, "Guido Laurin," *Biographie nationale de Belgique* (Brussels, 1866–1944), 11:col. 458.

5. "Mark Laurin," *Nationaal biografisch woordenboek*, ed. J. Duwerger (Brussels, 1977), 7:cols. 500–501.

6. Max Bruchet, *Archives départmentales du Nord, répertoire numerique*, vol. 2, série B (Lille, 1921), pp. 200–201; Henri Pirenne, *Histoire de Belgique* (Brussels, 1912), 3:266, n. 1; "Mark Laurin," *Nationaal biografisch woordenboek*, 7:col. 501. The Ghent, Rijksuniversitet, Centrale Bibliotheek, MS 181(1) is a parchment map showing polder areas belonging to Jérôme and his family.

7. L. P. Gachard, *Collection des voyages des souverains des Pay-Bas* (Brussels, 1876), 1:468–70.

8. Document B6777, Archives du Nord; Document 7948, Chambre des Comptes, Archives Générales du Royaume.

9. Alexandre Henne, *Histoire de regne de Charles-Quint* (Brussels, 1858), 1:136, n. 4; Ghislaine de Boom, *Marguerite d'Autriche-Savoie et la Pré Renaissance* (Paris, 1935), pp. 118 and 120.

10. Remarks in Documents 7141, fol. 11, and 17425, fol. 7, Archives Générales du Royaume, indicate that Jérôme had died by December 1509. Documents B2215, section 75680; B2225, section 76334; and B2226, section 76511, Archives du Nord (payments of Lauweryn's bequest to his heirs by Maximilian and Charles V, Philip the Handsome's son), verify that Jérôme had died between 29 May 1509 and 15 July 1510. L. Devliegher, "Het Graf van Hieronymus Lauweryn te Watervliet," *Handelingen van het genootschap voor geschiedenis gesticht onder de benaming Société d'Emulation to Brugge* 97 (1960): 100, 102, notes that Jérôme drew up his testament on 21 July 1509 and requested to be buried in the church he founded in Watervliet. Devliegher also suggests that the date 1 August 1509 inscribed on Jérôme's tomb may be the actual death date.

11. Georges van Doorslaer, "La Chapelle musicale de Philippe le Beau," *Revue belge d'archéologie et d'histoire de l'art* 4 (1934): 53–54.

12. Roersch, "Guido Laurin," col. 459; Vocht, *Collegium Trilingue Louvaniense*, 2:68.

13. Roersch, "Guido Laurin," cols. 461–62.

14. Ibid., cols. 467–68; Vocht, *Collegium Trilingue Louvaniense*, 3:320.

15. Helen Hewitt, "*Fors seulement* and the Cantus Firmus Technique of the Fifteenth Century," in *Essays in Musicology in Honor of Dragan Plamenac on His 70th Birthday*, ed. Gustave Reese and Robert J. Snow (Pittsburgh, 1969), pp. 91–126, and Martin Picker, ed., *Fors seulement: Thirty Compositions for Three to Five Voices or Instruments from the Fifteenth and Sixteenth Centuries*, Recent Researches in the Music of the Middle Ages and Early Renaissance, vol. 14 (Madison, Wis., 1981).

16. See Howard M. Brown's discussion of this genre in "The *Chanson rustique*: Popular Elements in the 15th- and 16th-Century Chanson," *Journal of the American Musicological Society* 12 (Spring 1959): 16–26.

17. Ibid., p. 19.

18. Howard M. Brown, "The Genesis of a Style: The Parisian Chanson, 1500–1530," in *Chanson and Madrigal, 1480–1530, Studies in Comparison and Contrast*, ed. James Haar (Cambridge, Mass., 1964), p. 20.

19. Brown, "The *Chanson rustique*," pp. 20–23, and *Music in the French Secular Theater, 1400–1550* (Cambridge, Mass., 1963), pp. 119–31, discusses these styles in addition to an earlier "double chanson" category.

20. Brown, "The *Chanson rustique*," p. 22.

21. Ibid., p. 24.

22. Ibid., pp. 24–25; Lawrence F. Bernstein, "The 'Parisian Chanson': Problems of Style and Terminology," *Journal of the American Musicological Society* 31 (Summer 1978): 193–240, focuses on the diversity of chanson styles (of which the Claudin type is one) promulgated in the printed collections of Pierre Attaingnant, the royal printer of Paris in the second quarter of the sixteenth century.

23. Brown, "The Genesis of a Style," p. 33, suggests that Claudin's earliest chansons were three-voice settings, thus strengthening the relationship to the homophonic pieces of the edition.

24. Brown, "The *Chanson rustique*," p. 24.

25. François Lesure, "Les Chansons à trois voix de Clément Janequin," *Revue de musicologie* 44 (1959): 193–98.

26. Brown, "The *Chanson rustique*," p. 25, and "The Genesis of a Style," p. 22.

27. Helmuth Osthoff, *Josquin Desprez* (Tutzing, 1965), 2:182–83, and Jaap van Benthem, "Josquin's Three-part 'Chansons rustiques': A Critique of the Readings in Manuscripts and Prints," *Josquin des Prez: Proceedings of the International Josquin Festival-Conference Held at the Julliard School, Lincoln Center, New York City, June, 1971* (London, 1976), p. 423, n. 10, reject the attribution to Josquin and acknowledge Févin as the composer.

28. Courtney Adams, "Some Aspects of the Chanson for Three Voices during the Sixteenth Century," *Acta musicologica* 49 (1977): 232, n. 15, and p.233, points out the relationship between the three anonymous works and the Parisian chanson style and notes that these pieces antedate Attaingnant's earliest prints by nearly two decades. She concludes that such three-voice *chansons rustiques* can be considered early Parisian chansons as well.

29. Margery Anthea Baird, ed., *Pierre de Manchicourt: Twenty-Nine Chansons*, Recent Researches in the Music of the Renaissance, vol. 11 (Madison, Wis., 1972), pp. xiii–xiv.

30. J. E. Mansion, *Harrap's New Standard French and English Dictionary*, ed. R.P.L. and Margaret Ledesert (London, 1972).

31. Louise Litterick, "Performing Franco-Netherlandish Secular Music of the Late 15th Century," *Early Music* 8 (1980): 474–85, concludes that the presence or absence of texts in French, Burgundian, and Italian sources of the late fifteenth and early sixteenth centuries is not the result of scribal whims, but indications of varying local performance practices.

Critical Commentary

Information on each piece is arranged in the following order: concordances, including manuscripts, early printed collections, modern editions, and intabulations; type of composition; related compositions; commentary to the text; and commentary to the transcription. In the commentary on the related compositions, pieces from other sources which have both a musical and textual relationship in this edition are cited for nine chansons of the edition (nos. 3, 5, 6, 7, 10, 11, 12, 16, and 19), and works which have only a textual relationship are listed for three other compositions in the anthology (nos. 14, 22, and 23). In the textual commentary, variants occuring in the first stanza are cited by measure-number, while those in succeeding stanzas are indicated by line-number. Unless otherwise indicated, the text variant cited affects all voice parts in a given piece. Lotrian 1543, Paris 1274, and Jeffery, *Chanson Verse*, three sources cited in the commentary to the text, contain texts only and are therefore not listed among the music concordances. Two monophonic sources with texts, Paris 9346 and Paris 12744, and their published versions, Gérold, *Manuscrit de Bayeux*, and Paris-Gevaert, *Chansons*, are also cited in the commentary to the text. As sources for the monophonic melodic models for the polyphonic chansons of the edition, these collections are listed under the "type of composition" category. In the commentary to the transcription, initial citations are made by measure-number. Beat-number citations refer to quarter-note beats in the transcriptions. Pitches are cited according to the Helmholtz system of pitch designation, wherein middle C = c′, the C above middle C = c″, and so forth. All variants are from London Add. 35087 unless otherwise indicated. Sources are identified by *sigla* explained in Appendix A: Sources. Voice classifications are abbreviated: S = superius; T = tenor; CT = contratenor; A = altus; B = bassus.

[1] *Adieu m'amour du temps passé*

Anon.; 3 voices; fols. 9ᵛ–10.

CONCORDANCES
None.

TYPE OF COMPOSITION
Chanson rustique based on an unknown popular monophonic melody.

RELATED COMPOSITIONS
None.

COMMENTARY TO THE TEXT
One stanza of text in each voice. Mm. 6 and 9, CT has "voz." Mm. 8–9, CT has "sayson." Mm. 12–19, all voices, "congiet . . . donné" = "donner congé" may be translated as "to give leave (a holiday)." Mm. 21–22, T has "rayson." M. 25, CT has "say." Mm. 36–37, CT has "aves." Mm. 38–39, T has "prendes." Mm. 39–40, S has "prenes."

COMMENTARY TO THE TRANSCRIPTION
No variants.

[2] *Amy, l'aurez vous donc, fortune*

Anon.; 3 voices; fols. 89ᵛ–90.

CONCORDANCES
Manuscript
Uppsala 76a, fol. 21ᵛ; anon.; *a 3*; S with text; this setting contains a *secunda pars*.

TYPE OF COMPOSITION
Chanson musicale.

RELATED COMPOSITIONS
None.

COMMENTARY TO THE TEXT
One stanza of text in each voice. Mm. 16–18, T has "que ay chosy." Mm. 20–21, CT has "chosy." Mm. 33–35, S has "Quar tousjours l'ay aymée" ("For I have always loved her") in Uppsala 76a. M. 34, T has "toujours"; CT lacks "l'ay."

The heterometric second stanza is taken from Uppsala 76a. L. 2, "solas" may be translated as "diversion." L. 3, "rent" is a variant of "rang." L. 4, "ne . . . oncques" is equivalent to "ne . . . jamais."

COMMENTARY TO THE TRANSCRIPTION
All variants listed here are those between London Add. 35087 and the *prima pars* of Uppsala 76a; there are no variants between the edition *(prima pars)* and London Add. 35087. M. 2, T, note is a half-note and two beats are lacking. M. 20, CT, note 1 is a half-note and note 2 is a quarter-note. M. 20, beat 3–m. 21, beat 2, S, a′ and c″, quarter-notes, with two beats lacking. M. 28–m. 29, beat 2, CT, rhythm is as follows.

M. 29, CT, note 1 is b-natural. M. 34, beats 1–4, T, whole-note (c′). M. 35, beat 1–m. 36, beat 2, CT, dotted whole-note (c). M. 39, T, note 2 is an eighth-note, and thus one beat is lacking.

[3] Buvons, ma comere, et nous ne buvons point!

Benedictus Appe[n]sc[h]elders; 3 voices; fols. 78ᵛ–79.

CONCORDANCES
Modern Edition
Thompson, *Appenzeller*, Appendix I, p. 297 (after London Add. 35087).

TYPE OF COMPOSITION
Chanson rustique based on a popular monophonic melody, one version of which appears in Paris 9346, fol. 15ᵛ (published in Gérold, *Manuscrit de Bayeux*, no. 15).

RELATED COMPOSITIONS
The following compositions are based on the same *cantus prius factus*; they are different from the London Add. 35087 setting and from each other.

1. London Add. 19583, fol. 46; P. Gauvain; A only with text. Modena α F.2.29, p. 11; anon.; T only with text.

2. Le Roy and Ballard 1553²², fol. 11ᵛ; Gascongne; *a 3*; text in all voices. Modern Edition: Adams, *Three-Part Chanson*, 2:493; Gascongne (after Le Roy and Ballard 1553²²).

COMMENTARY TO THE TEXT
One stanza of text in each voice. Mm. 1–2, S and T have "buvon"; Paris 9346 reads "bevon." Mm. 2–4, Paris 9346 gives "commere." M. 4, Paris 9346 lacks "et." M. 6, Paris 9346 reads "bevons." Mm. 8–13, Paris 9346 has "Ilz estoient trois dames d'acord et d'apoint," with the result that all lines end in "point," which offers a possible obscene play on words, the nuances of which are impossible to translate. M. 11, S lacks "en." Mm. 14–16, Paris 9346 has "l'ung à l'aultre" for "ma comere." M. 17, S lacks "buvons." Mm. 17–18, Paris 9346 has "bevons." M. 23, Paris 9346 reads "bevons."

Paris 9346 adds five more stanzas. L. 19, the "e" of "De" is elided in Gérold, *Manuscrit de Bayeux*.

COMMENTARY TO THE TRANSCRIPTION
No variants.

[4] C'est donc par moy qu'ainsy suis fortunée?

[Ninot le Petit]; 3 voices; fols. 81ᵛ–83.

CONCORDANCES
Manuscripts
Cambrai 125–128, fol. 19; anon.; *a 4*; text in all voices.

Heilbronn X. 2, no. 1; Adrianus Wilhart; B only, with incipit "Ce danc par moy."

London Add. 29381, fol. 35ᵛ; Ninon le Petit; *a 3*; text in all voices.

Munich 1516, no. 133; anon.; *a 3*; incipit "Cest dont pour moy" in all voices.

Ulm 237ᵃ⁻ᵈ, S: fol. 21ᵛ, T: fol. 19, CT: fol. 20; anon.; *a 3*; incipits "Cest doy pari moy" in S and "Cest doy par moy" in T and CT.

Early Printed Collections
Egenolff [c. 1535]¹⁴, III, no. 47; anon.; S only, with incipit "Cedant."

Formschneider 1538⁹, no. 61; anon.; *a 3*.

Gardane 1541¹³, p. 60; Janequin (attribution in title of the printed collection); *a 3*; text in all voices.

Gardane 1543²³, p. 52; Janequin (attribution in title of the printed collection); *a 3*; T only, with text.

Modern Editions
Maldeghem, *Trésor musical*, 15 (1879): 20; attributed to Benedictus Hertoghs [Appenzeller] with text "Grootmachtig God!" (after Cambrai 125–128).

Whisler, *Munich 1516*, 2:345; Appenzeller (after Munich 1516).

Intabulations
Brown, *Instrumental Music Printed before 1600*, lists 1545₃, p. 34, no. 31; 1547₇, fol. D₃v, no. 22.

TYPE OF COMPOSITION
Chanson musicale.

RELATED COMPOSITIONS
None.

COMMENTARY TO THE TEXT
One stanza of text in each voice. M. 6, CT reads "que ainsy." Mm. 6–8, London Add. 29381 has "qu'ainsis." M. 7, S has "qu'ainsi." Mm. 7–8, S and T of Cambrai 125–128 read "que je" instead of "qu'ainsy." Mm. 9–10, S has "qu'ainsi." M. 9, note 2–m. 12, S has no text in London Add. 29381. Mm. 13–14, S reads "hellas," an obvious error, in London Add. 29381. Mm. 15–17, CT reads "infortunée, helas." Mm. 22–25, this line is lacking in T of London Add. 35087, Cambrai 125–128, London Add. 29381, Gardane 1541¹³, and Gardane 1543²³. Mm. 26–28, London Add. 29381 has "malheureusse" and "malheureuse," Gardane 1541¹³ has "malheureuse," Gardane 1543²³ reads "malheurese." Mm. 29–31, T has "ne cognoy," CT reads "ne cognoys"; London Add. 29381, Gardane 1541¹³, and Gardane 1543²³ read "n'est que moy," with no change in meaning. Mm. 32–33, CT has "ne cognoy." Mm. 35–36, CT reads "ne cognoy." Mm. 41–42, all voices, London 29381 reads "telle" instead of "tel." M. 48, all parts, Cambrai 125–128 reads "ne fust" (past tense of "n'est"). Mm. 48–49, T and London 29381 have "telle."

In this *chanson débat*, each lover claims to be more miserable than the other. Mm. 1–14, mm. 22–25, and mm. 37–51 refer to the woman (note the feminine endings: "fortunée," "infortunée," "née"), and mm. 12–22 and mm. 26–37 refer to the man (note the masculine endings: "infortuné" and "malheureux").

COMMENTARY TO THE TRANSCRIPTION
M. 1–m. 2, beat 2, S, dotted whole-note in Form-

schneider 1538[9]. M. 3–m. 4, beat 2, CT, dotted whole-note in Ulm 237[a–d] and Formschneider 1538[9]. M. 3, beat 3–m. 4, beat 2, S, two half-notes in Munich 1516. M. 5, CT, two half-notes (e, e) in Heilbronn X. 2.; T, note 2 is a in Formschneider 1538[9]. M. 8, CT, notes 3 and 4, two quarter-notes (d, e) in Heilbronn X. 2.; T, note 4 is b in Formschneider 1538[9]. M. 10, beats 1–2, CT, two quarter-notes (f, f) in Munich 1516, Gardane 1541[13], and London Add. 29381 (where note values are reduced by half for these variant readings). M. 10, beat 4–m. 11, beat 1, S, two quarter-notes; amended to read half-note (c″) after other sources for the sake of the text. M. 11, beat 3–m. 12, beat 1, S, half-note, quarter-note in Ulm 237[a–d]. M. 15, beats 1–2, T, half-note (e′) in Formschneider 1538[9]; S, beats 2–4, dotted half-note (b′) in Formschneider 1538[9]. M. 16, beat 3–m. 17, beat 2, S, two half-notes in Munich 1516; CT, whole-note (a) in Formschneider 1538[9]. M. 17, T, note 1 is a dotted half-note in London Add. 29381 and Gardane 1541[13]. M. 17, beat 3–m. 18, beat 1, S, dotted half-note (b′) in London Add. 29381 and Gardane 1541[13]. M. 18, beats 1–2, T, half-note (e′) in Formschneider 1538[9]; S, beats 3–4, half-note (b′) in Formschneider 1538[9]; CT, beats 3–4, half-note (g) in Formschneider 1538[9]. M. 19, beats 1–2, CT, half-note (d) in Cambrai 125–128, Heilbronn X. 2., London Add. 29381, Munich 1516, Ulm 237[a–d], and Gardane 1541[13]. M. 19, beat 3–m. 20, beat 2, T, two half-notes in Ulm 237[a–d]. M. 20, beat 4–m. 21, beat 2, CT, three quarter-notes (e, d, c) in Heilbronn X. 2. M. 21, S, whole-note (a′) in Cambrai 125–128, Egenolff [c. 1535][14], and Formschneider 1538[9]; T, whole-note (f′) in Formschneider 1538[9]; CT, beats 3–4, two quarter-notes (d, d) in London Add. 29381, Ulm 237[a–d], and Gardane 1541[13]. M. 23, note 4–m. 24, note 2, S, half-note (b′) in Cambrai 125–128, Ulm 237[a–d], and Formschneider 1538[9]. M. 23, beat 4–m. 24, beat 3, S, four quarter-notes (b′, b′, a′, a′) in London Add. 29381 and Gardane 1541[13]. M. 24, beats 2–3, S, dotted quarter-note (a′) and eighth-note (g′) in Egenolff [c. 1535][14]; CT, beats 3–4, two quarter-notes (e, e) in Heilbronn X. 2., London Add. 29381, Munich 1516, and Gardane 1541[13]. M. 26, beat 3–m. 27, beat 2, S, dotted half-note (e′), quarter-note (f′) in Egenolff [c. 1535][14]; T, whole-note (c′) in Formschneider 1538[9]. M. 27, beats 1–2, S, half-note (e′) in Formschneider 1538[9]. M. 28, beats 1–3, S, half-note and quarter-rest in Cambrai 125–128 and Munich 1516; T, beats 2–3, two quarter-notes (g′, g′) in Munich 1516 and Gardane 1541[13]. M. 28, beat 4–m. 29, beat 1, CT, half-note (g) in Formschneider 1538[9]. M. 30, S, note 1 is a dotted quarter and notes 2–3 are sixteenths in Egenolff [c. 1535][14]; T, note 2 is e′ in London Add. 29381. M. 30, beat 4–m. 31, beat 1, T, half-note (d′) in Formschneider 1538[9]. M. 31, beat 4–m. 32, beat 1, CT, half-note (g) in Formschneider 1538[9]. M. 32, T, note 2 is a quarter and notes 3–4 are eighths in Cambrai 125–128, and notes 2–4 are half-notes (c′) in Ulm 237[a–d], Formschneider 1538[9],

and Gardane 1543[23]. M. 34, T, note 4 is e′ in Cambrai 125–128. M. 34, beat 4–m. 35, beat 1, CT, half-note (g) in Formschneider 1538[9]. M. 35, beats 3–4, T, two quarter-notes (d′, d′) in London Add. 29381, Munich 1516, and Gardane 1541[13]. M. 39, CT, note 1 is a dotted quarter and notes 2–3 are sixteenth-notes in Heilbronn X. 2. M. 42, S, note 2 is c″ in Egenolff [c. 1535][14]. M. 43, beat 1, S, two eighth-notes (b′, a′) in Cambrai 125–128; T, beats 3–4, two quarter-notes (b, b) in Munich 1516. M. 47, beat 4, T, two eighth-notes (c′, b) in London Add. 29381 and Gardane 1541[13]. M. 49, S, notes 1 and 2 are dotted quarter-note and eighth-note in Cambrai 125–128 and Ulm 237[a–d], and notes 4 and 5 are b′ and a′ in Cambrai 125–128; CT, beats 3–4 are four eighth-notes (c, d, e, f) in Cambrai 125–128, Heilbronn X. 2., and Munich 1516. M. 49, beat 4–m. 50, beat 2, T, dotted quarter-note (e′), eighth-note (d′), and quarter-note (c′) in Cambrai 125–128; CT, half-note (g) and quarter-note (f) in Formschneider 1538[9]. M. 50, beats 2–4, S, half-note (a′) and quarter-note (g′) in London Add. 29381, Munich 1516, Egenolff [c. 1535][14], Formschneider 1538[9], and Gardane 1541[13], and quarter-note (a′) and four eighth-notes (g′, f′, a′, g′) in Ulm 237[a–d]; S, beat 4, eighth-note (g′) and two sixteenth-notes (f′, g′) in Cambrai 125–128.

[5] Coment peult avoir joye

Jo. de Vyzeto; 4 voices; fols. 36[v]–37.

Three voices given with one stanza of text in each; the direction "In dyatessaron" placed above S and a *signum* in that voice indicate the entry of a fourth canonic voice. A facsimile of this setting appears in Hewitt, *Canti B,* p. 47.

CONCORDANCES
None.

TYPE OF COMPOSITION
Chanson rustique and German *Lied* "Wohlauf, gut G'sell, von hinnen!" based on an unknown popular monophonic melody.

RELATED COMPOSITIONS
French and German compositions are all based on the same *cantus prius factus.* Hewitt, *Canti B,* pp. 46–49, discusses the Franco-German tune and Josquin's use of it and provides a list of concordances for both French and German settings. Her commentary is based in part on the study by Helmuth Osthoff, " 'Wohlauf, gut G'sell, von hinnen!': Ein Beispiel deutsch-französischer Liedgemeinschaft um 1500," *Jahrbuch für Volksliedforschung* 8 (1951): 122–36. Since Hewitt and Osthoff have examined the German settings, which have no textual relationship to the French setting of this edition, only the French pieces (one with Latin substituted) are listed below; they are all different from the London Add. 35087 setting and from each other.

1. Bologna Q 17, fol. 58[v]; Josquin; *a 4;* incipit "Co-

ment peult avoir Joye" in three given voices; the direction "Fuga duorum temporum dyapason" placed to the left of S and a *signum* in that voice indicate the entry of a fourth canonic voice. Florence 178, fol. 7ᵛ; Josquin; *a 4;* incipit "cOmen potaver yoye" in highest of three given voices; a *signum* in S indicates the entry of a fourth canonic voice. Rome C. G. XIII.27, fol. 4ᵛ (fol. 11ᵛ); Josquin Despres; *a 4;* incipit "Ne come peult" in highest of three given voices; a *signum* in the S indicates the entry of a fourth canonic voice; Atlas, *The Cappella Giulia Chansonnier,* 1:60, furnishes a list of concordances for this setting. Petrucci 1502²², fol. 22ᵛ; Josquin; *a 4;* incipit "Coment peult haver joye" in S and A of four voices. Egenolff [c. 1535]¹⁴, I, no. 27; anon.; S only, with incipit "Coment peult haver ioye." Glareanus 1547¹, p. 356; Jodocus Pratensis; *a 4;* Latin text "O Jesu fili David" (from Matt. 15: 22, 26, and 28) substituted in all voices. Modern Editions: Hewitt, *Canti B,* p. 145; Josquin (after Petrucci 1502²); Josquin, *Wereldlijke Werken,* ser. 4, vol. 5:18 (after Bologna R 142, Florence 178, Rome C. G. XIII.27, Petrucci 1502², Egenolff [c. 1535]¹⁴, and Glareanus 1547¹); Miller, *Heinrich Glarean, Dodecachordon,* 2:434; Josquin des Prez (after Glareanus 1547¹). Intabulation: Brown, *Instrumental Music Printed before 1600,* lists 1507₂, fol. 19ᵛ, no. 14.

2. Bologna Q 18, fol. 68ᵛ; anon.; *a 3;* incipit "Coment peult" in all voices. Rome C. G. XIII.27, fol. 110ᵛ (fol. 117ᵛ); Ysach; *a 3;* incipit "Coment poit avoir yoye" in S; Atlas, *The Cappella Giulia Channsonnier,* 1:222–26, discusses Isaac's French, German, and Latin settings of the melody. Modern Edition: Isaac, *Weltliche Werke,* 28: 66 (after Rome C. G. XIII.27).

3. Egenolff [c. 1535]¹⁴, III, no. 50; anon.; S only, with incipit "Comment."

COMMENTARY TO THE TEXT

In the following commentary, S, T, and CT refer to the original lower voices. Mm. 3–4, T reads "avoer." Mm. 6–11, line is lacking and supplied by Florence 164–167. Hewitt, *Canti B,* pp. 47–48, establishes the need for this extra line in the London Add. 35087 text to produce eight lines with rhyme scheme abab cdcd. Citing the corrupted French text of an Italian quodlibet in the text source Florence 164–167 (after Bianca Becherini, "Tre incatenature del codice fiorentino Magl. XIX. 164–65–66–67," *Collectanea historiae musicae,* 1 [Florence, L. S. Olschki, 1953]) as the source for the missing line, Hewitt substitutes "Qui fortune content," the French equivalent for the quodlibet's "che fortune content." Lotrian 1543, fol. 90ᵛ, lists *Coment peult avoir joye qui fortune contrainct* as the title of a chanson melody and then provides a different text, "une jeune fillette en l'aage de quinze ans," to be sung to the melody. However, the Lotrian 1543 title substantiates the addition of the second line to the London Add. 35087 text. M. 11, CT has "l'osiau." M. 12, CT has

"per." M. 13, T reads "l'oysiaux." Mm. 17–22, line is lacking in S and T; all voices, "neus" is equivalent to "nous." Mm. 22–23, CT gives "au bois." Mm. 23–24, T reads "a bois." Mm. 24–25, instead of "ramée," CT reads "bordure," which in context means "at the edge of the woods"; Hewitt, *Canti B,* p. 48, reads "verdure" in the CT, which she uses for her reading, and lists "ramée" as a variant. M. 26, T reads, "n'ay." Mm. 27–30, T has "sez desirs."

COMMENTARY TO THE TRANSCRIPTION
No variants.

[6] Dieu gard de mal de deshonneur

[Jean Mouton]; 3 voices; fols. 91ᵛ–93.

CONCORDANCES
Manuscript
Cambridge 1760, fol. 68ᵛ; Jo. Mouton; *a 3;* text in all voices.

TYPE OF COMPOSITION

Chanson rustique based on a popular monophonic melody, one version of which appears in Paris 9346, fol. 32ᵛ (published in Gérold, *Manuscrit de Bayeux,* no. 32). An unrelated melody with a similar first stanza of text appears in Paris 12744, fol. 24 (published in Paris-Gevaert, *Chansons,* no. 33).

RELATED COMPOSITION

The following composition is based on the same *cantus prius factus;* it is different from the London Add. 35087 setting.

London Harley 5242, fol. 45ᵛ; anon.; *a 3;* text "Dieu gard celle de deshonneur" in all voices.

COMMENTARY TO THE TEXT

One stanza of text in each voice. Our source has only six lines of text; Cambridge 1760 and London Harley 5242 contain one eight-line stanza each. Paris 9346 and Gérold, *Manuscrit de Bayeux,* furnish two stanzas; Paris 1274, fol. 68ᵛ, gives four stanzas, and Paris 12744 and Paris-Gevaert, *Chansons,* have three eight-line stanzas. Note the anomaly in all sources of eight- and six-syllable lines, which do not appear in alternating order. Mm. 1–11, London Harley 5242 and Paris 9346 read "Dieu gard celle de deshonneur," which preserves the same meaning. Mm. 9–14, "celle" is lacking in London Harley 5242, Paris 1274, Paris 9346, and Paris 12744. Mm. 14–20, Paris 1274 reads "je" for "j'ay." Mm. 14–17, "longtemps" is lacking in T and CT of Cambridge 1760. Mm. 27–35, text underlay follows Cambridge 1760, Harley 5242, and Paris 9346 for better meaning; T and CT of London Add. 35087 read "Car elle m'a dit en plorant / Vous amours sont finées"; S lacks text. Mm. 27–31, Paris 1274 and Paris 12744 read "Avec elle par grand dou[l]ceur," meaning "With her in sweet pleasure." Mm. 31–35, Cambridge 1760 gives "Mes amours sont finées." M. 36, T reads "voeye."

Mm. 38–39, T and CT give "follye," London Harley 5242 reads, "foleur," and Paris 1274, Paris 9346, and Paris 12744 give "folleur." Mm. 39–40, Paris 1274 reads "mettre plus," with no change in meaning; Paris 12744 has "d'y avoir," which changes the meaning of the line: "To have thought of it." M. 41, T and CT, London Harley 5242 and Paris 9346 have "sa"—both *ma* and *sa* can be used interchangeably in this context; they imply that the lover is simply referring to himself in the third person. Mm. 44–47, Cambridge 1760, London Harley 5242, and Paris 9346 read "quant" for "car," which changes "when" to "for." Mm. 44–54, Paris 1274 gives "Puysqu'el[le] a faiz amy ailleurs," meaning "Since she has found a friend elsewhere," and Paris 12744 has "Puis qu'elle m'a dit par rigueur," meaning "Since she told me in fact." Mm. 45–48, T and CT give "m'a dyt." Mm. 52–56, all voices read "vous" for "nos"; the text is amended after London Harley 5242 and Paris 9346 to provide the first person plural form required by the meaning of the text. Mm. 52–70, Cambridge 1760 gives "Vostre amour est finée," Paris 12744 has "Nostre amour est finée," and Paris 1274 reads "De moy s'est eslongée," meaning "[She] has left me."

The second stanza appears in Paris 9346; the third stanza of Paris 1274 differs from the second stanza of Paris 9346 in this manner only; in place of "Payer l'escot de maincte gent / Dont je n'en avoys pas mestier," Paris 1274 reads "En compagnye et mainte gen / Tout je n'avoys pas mestier," meaning "In the company of many people / That I had no use for." The second and fourth stanzas of Paris 1274, which on p. 19 of the present edition follow the second stanza, differ from Paris 9346 as follows: L. 3 of Paris 1274 gives "g'ay," the equivalent of "j'ay." L. 10, Paris 1274 has "piurest" as one word, which should probably read "qui est piur est[at] aux amoureux," with the elision of "at" before "aux." The line expresses a common theme: "which is a worse state for lovers." L. 13 of Paris 1274, "semaindieux" means "holy week," a mild swear word. L. 15 of Paris 1274, "s'y aille" is equivalent to "s'en aille."

Paris 12744 provides a second stanza that differs slightly from the Paris 1274 stanza given here. For example, l. 1 of Paris 12744 has "A pourpenser je me suis mys," and Paris 1274 has "Je me suys mis à pourpenser." L. 13, Paris-Gevaert, *Chansons* (after Paris 12744), gives "dueil" for "douleur." The third stanza of Paris 12744 differs more noticeably from Paris 1274.

Commentary to the Transcription
Unless otherwise indicated, variants cited are those between the edition and London Add. 35087. However, many variants are listed from Cambridge 1760, where the positions of S and T are switched: S appears on the recto side above the CT, whereas T appears on the verso side. Emendations have been made in the edition for the sake of the text underlay. M. 1, beats 1–

3, CT, dotted half-note (c'). M. 4, beats 1–3, T, dotted half-note (g'); CT, half-note (g) and quarter-note (g) in Cambridge 1760. M. 11, beat 4–m. 12, beat 1, CT, half-note (c') in Cambridge 1760. M. 15, beats 2–4, CT, half-note (g) and quarter-note (g) in Cambridge 1760. M. 17, beat 2, CT, two eighth-notes (g, f) in Cambridge 1760. M. 20, note 5–m. 21, note 2, T, half-note (d') in Cambridge 1760. M. 26, beat 1, S, quarter-note (a') in Cambridge 1760. M. 27, beat 3–m. 28, beat 1, CT, dotted half-note (g). M. 28, beats 1–3, T, dotted half-note (d'). M. 31, beat 3–m. 32, beat 1, CT, half-note and quarter-note in Cambridge 1760. M. 32, beats 1–3, T, half-note (c') and quarter-note (c') in Cambridge 1760. M. 33, beat 4–m. 34, beat 1, T, two quarter-notes (d', c') in Cambridge 1760. M. 36, S, note 1 is f' in Cambridge 1760. M. 42, beats 1–4, S, whole-note (f') in Cambridge 1760. M. 44, beats 1–3, CT, dotted half-note (c'). M. 44, beat 3–m. 45, beat 1, S, dotted half-note (g'). M. 47, beats 1–3, T, dotted half-note (g'); CT, half-note (g) and quarter-note (g) in Cambridge 1760. M. 49, beat 1–m. 50, beat 4, T, this passage missing in Cambridge 1760. M. 54, beat 4–m. 55, beat 2, CT, dotted half-note (c') in London Add. 35087 and Cambridge 1760. M. 58, beats 2–4, CT, three quarter-notes (g, g, g) in Cambridge 1760. M. 60, beat 2, CT, two eighth-notes (g, f) in Cambridge 1760. M. 61, beat 4–m. 62, beat 2, CT, three quarter-notes (f, f, f) in Cambridge 1760. M. 67, beat 2, CT, two eighth-notes (g, f) in Cambridge 1760. M. 69, beat 1, S, two eighth-notes (a', d') in Cambridge 1760.

[7] Du bon du cueur ma chiere dame

Anon.; 3 voices; fols. 4ᵛ–5.

Concordances
Manuscripts
Munich 1503ᵃ, no. 4; anon.; *a 3*; incipit "Du bon du ceur" in all voices.
Munich 1516, no. 138; anon.; *a 3*; incipit "Du bon du ceur" in all voices.
Ulm 237ᵃ⁻ᵈ, no. 36; anon.; *a 3*; incipits "Du bon du cuer" in S and "Du bon cuer" in T and B.

Early Printed Collection
Formschneider 1538⁹, no. 9; anon.; *a 3*.

Modern Edition
Whisler, *Munich 1516*, 2:355; anon. (after Munich 1516).

Intabulations
Brown, *Instrumental Music Printed before 1600*, lists 1545₃, p. 36, no. 32; and 1547₇, fol. D₄ᵛ, no. 23.

Type of Composition
Chanson musicale.

Related Compositions
The following compositions are based on the same *cantus prius factus.* They are different from the London Add. 35087 setting and from each other.

1. Vienna 18746, no. 32; anon.; *a 5;* incipits "Du bon du coeur" in T, A, and *Seconda Tenor,* "Du boen deu couer" in S, and "Du bon du cuer" in B. Le Roy and Ballard 1572[2], fol. 45; Mouton; *a 5;* text in all voices.

2. Susato 1545[14], fol. 14[v]; Philippe de Vuildre; *a 6;* text in all voices.

COMMENTARY TO THE TEXT
One stanza of text in each voice. Mm. 3–4, T has "cuer." Mm. 5–6, CT reads "ceur." Mm. 7–9, S gives "couer." Mm. 11–15, Le Roy and Ballard 1572[2] adds "Je vous serviray loyaument" before the second text line in the S only, and all voices of Le Roy and Ballard 1572[2] and Susato 1545[14] substitute "Je vous supply[e] tres humblement" for the second text line. Mm. 16–19, T has "recheves" and CT gives both "recheves" and "rechevez," and T and CT of Le Roy and Ballard 1572[2] and Susato 1545[14] have "recevés." Mm. 18–22, S of Le Roy and Ballard 1572[2] gives "retenez," meaning "keep me in your service." Mm. 20–24, CT has "douchement." Mm. 22–24, S reads "doulchement," and Le Roy and Ballard 1572[2] gives "doucement." Mm. 29–34, Susato 1545[14] and Le Roy and Ballard 1572[2] read "Et si vous jure sur mon ame," meaning "And so I swear to you on my soul." Mm. 34 and 37, T has "voz." M. 37, CT reads "voz." Mm. 34–40, Susato 1545[14] has "Que je vous serviray leallement." Mm. 35–40, T and CT have "leaulment," Susato 1545[14] gives "leallement," and Le Roy and Ballard 1572[2] has "loyaument."

COMMENTARY TO THE TRANSCRIPTION
M. 3, T, note 1 is a dotted quarter-note in Formschneider 1538[9], which is an error. M. 7, beats 2–3, T, quarter-note (d') and two eighth-notes (d', c'); emended after Munich 1503[a], Munich 1516, and Formschneider 1538[9] to eliminate the repetition of (d') on a vowel in the text. M. 7, beat 4–m. 8, beat 1, CT, half-note (e-natural) in Ulm 237[a–d]. M. 9, S, note 1 is a dotted half and note 2 is a quarter-note in Ulm 237[a–d], and beats 1–4 are whole-note (f') in Formschneider 1538[9]. M. 12, beats 2–4, S, dotted half-note (a') in Formschneider 1538[9]; CT, note 2 is g in Munich 1516. M. 12, beat 3–m. 13, beat 1, T, half-note and quarter-note in Munich 1503[a] and Munich 1516. M. 13, CT, flat before note 1 in Formschneider 1538[9]. M. 15, beats 1–2, CT, half-note (f) in Ulm 237[a–d]. M. 15, beat 3–m. 16, beat 2, T, two half-notes in Munich 1516 and Formschneider 1538[9], and half-note with two beats lacking in Munich 1503[a]. M. 16, beat 3–m. 17, beat 2, S, two half-notes in Munich 1503[a], Munich 1516, and Formschneider 1538[9]; CT, whole-note (d) in Munich 1503[a], Munich 1516, and Ulm 237[a–d]. M. 19, note 4–m. 20, note 2, S, dotted quarter-note (a') and eighth-note (g') in Munich 1503[a], Munich 1516, and Formschneider 1538[9]. M. 20, beats 2–3, S, half-note (g') in Ulm 237[a–d]. M. 22, note 4–m. 23, note 2, S, two quarter-notes (b'-flat, b'-flat) in Munich 1503[a] and Munich 1516. M. 23, beats 2–

3, S, two quarter-notes (a', a') in Munich 1503[a]. M. 24, beats 2–3, CT, half-note (f) in Formschneider 1538[9]. M. 25, beats 1–2, T, half-note (c') in Formschneider 1538[9]. M. 28, T, note is lacking in Munich 1503[a]. M. 29, beats 1–3, S, dotted half-note (a') in Munich 1503[a], Munich 1516, and Formschneider 1538[9]; T, dotted half-note (c') in Formschneider 1538[9]; CT, dotted half-note (f) in Formschneider 1538[9]. M. 30, beats 1–4, CT, whole-note (f) in Formschneider 1538[9]; CT, note 2 is a in Munich 1503[a] and Munich 1516. M. 31, beats 1–4, T, two half-notes (d', d') in Munich 1503[a], Munich 1516, and Formschneider 1538[9]. M. 32, T, note 1 is a quarter-note with one beat lacking in Munich 1503[a]. M. 34, beats 1–2, CT, half-rest in Ulm 237[a–d]. M. 35, beats 1–2, T, two quarter-notes (b-flat, b-flat) in Ulm 237[a–d]. M. 38, beats 1–2, S, half-note (b'-flat) in Munich 1503[a], Munich 1516, and Formschneider 1538[9].

[8] *Fuyés regretz, avant que l'on s'avance*
Anthoine Fevin; 3 voices; fols. 88[v]–89.

CONCORDANCES
Modern Edition
Clinkscale, *Févin,* p. 460 (after London Add. 35087).

TYPE OF COMPOSITION
Chanson rustique based on an unknown popular monophonic melody.

RELATED COMPOSITIONS
None.

COMMENTARY TO THE TEXT
One stanza of text in each voice. Mm. 6–7, T reads "devant," an earlier form of "avant [que]." Mm. 16–18, T has "banyr." M. 29, T gives "que." M. 30, CT has "tous." Mm. 31–36, CT reads "faictz." Mm. 43–49, S and CT read "c'est."

COMMENTARY TO THE TRANSCRIPTION
S lacks three beats of music; a study of the cadences, the development of imitation, and the vertical alignment of voices indicates that this missing material must lie between mm. 22 and 28 of the transcription. Clinkscale, *Févin,* p. 460, suggests that omissions occur in m. 24, beat 4–m. 25, beat 2 (editor's numbers) and suggests a half-note (a') and two eighth-notes (g', f') to fill this gap. His solution fits smoothly into the structure of the composition at this point and has been adopted for the present edition.

[9] *Helas! dame que j'ayme tant*
Anon.; 3 voices; fols. 23[v]–24.

CONCORDANCES
None.

TYPE OF COMPOSITION
Chanson rustique dance song based on an unknown popular monophonic melody.

RELATED COMPOSITIONS
None.

COMMENTARY TO THE TEXT
One stanza of text in each voice. M. 1, T has "sçaves," and Jeffery, *Chanson Verse*, MS 11, reads "savez." M. 2, S and T have "qu'il i a," and CT lacks "qu'." Mm. 4–5, Jeffery, *Chanson Verse*, MS 11, reads "servir" for "jouir." M. 8, CT has "voz." M. 12, Jeffery, *Chanson Verse*, MS 11, reads "dueil." M. 13, T and CT have "paine." Jeffery, *Chanson Verse*, MS 11, provides the extra stanzas.

COMMENTARY TO THE TRANSCRIPTION
M. 2, S, beats 1–3, half-note (f') and quarter-note (f'); CT, note 1, half-note (d) and quarter-note (d), which have been emended for the sake of the first and third lines of text.

[10] Helas! pourquoy me sui ge mariée?

Anon.; 3 voices; fols. 79ᵛ–80.

CONCORDANCES
Manuscript
Paris 1597, fol. 39ᵛ; anon.; *a 3*; text in S and T; incipit "Helas pourquoy" in CT.

Modern Edition
Shipp, *Chansonnier of Dukes of Lorraine*, p. 399; anon. (after Paris 1597).

TYPE OF COMPOSITION
Chanson rustique based on an unknown popular monophonic melody.

RELATED COMPOSITION
The following composition is based on the same *cantus prius factus*; it is different from the London Add. 35087 setting.
Le Roy and Ballard 1572⁹, fol. 62; Leschenet; *a 6*; text in all voices.

COMMENTARY TO THE TEXT
One stanza of text in each voice. Mm. 1–10, Paris 1597 reads "Helas! pourquoy ne suys je maryee," and Le Roy and Ballard 1572² has "Helas! pourquoy ne suis je mariée," which translate as "Alas! Why am I not married?" M. 8, CT has "vrays." M. 8 in CT, m. 9 in S, m. 11 in T, Paris 1597 and Le Roy and Ballard 1572² add "Je viz[s] en dueil, en pleur[s], et en esmoy," meaning "I live in suffering, in tears, and in sorrow." M. 11, T reads "vray." Mm. 11–12, T has "amoreux." Mm. 11–16, S gives "prennez exemple, amy," meaning "friend, take me as an example," for "ayes de moy pité"; Le Roy and Ballard 1572² reads "ayes pitié de moy"; and Paris 1597 reads "souviengne vous de moy," meaning "remember me," the impersonal subjunctive construction. Mm. 16–24, Paris 1597 and Le Roy and Ballard 1572² offer a different line, "Et quelque jour, vous diray ma pensée," meaning "And someday, I'll tell you what I think." Mm. 24–36, where

all voices repeat "Helas! pourquoy me sui ge mariée," S follows with "me sui ge mariée"; T follows with "Helas! je suis desia lassée"; CT follows with "Hellas! pourquoy je suis desia lassée," meaning "Alas! Why, I am already tired of it!"; text underlay for the transcription here follows the repetition of "Helas! porquoy" from CT and the repetition of "me sui ge mariée" from S.

COMMENTARY TO THE TRANSCRIPTION
Except for one variant between the edition and London Add. 35087 (m. 27, CT), all other variants listed here are those between London Add. 35087 and Paris 1597. M. 2, beats 3–4, CT, dotted quarter-note (b-flat) and two sixteenth-notes (a, g). M. 4, S, note 1 is a dotted quarter-note and notes 2–3 are sixteenth-notes. M. 5, beat 3–m. 6, beat 2, CT, whole-note (g). M. 11, beats 1–4, S, dotted half-note (d") and two eighth-notes (c", b'-flat); CT, beats 3–4, half-note (g). M. 14, beat 4–m. 15, beat 1, S, dotted quarter-note (c") and eighth-note (b'-flat). M. 21, beat 1–m. 22, beat 2, CT, quarter-rest, three quarter-notes (f, f, f), and half-note (f). M. 22, beat 4–m. 23, beat 1, S, dotted quarter-note (a') and eighth-note (g'). M. 27, beats 3–4, CT, half-note (g) emended after Paris 1597 for the sake of the text underlay. M. 28, beat 4–m. 29, beat 1, S, dotted quarter-note (a') and eighth-note (g'). M. 33, beats 3–4, CT, half-note (g). M. 34, beat 4–m. 35, beat 1, S, dotted quarter-note (a') and eighth-note (g').

[11] James n'aymeray mason; je suis trop belle

Jo. [= Jean] Mouton; 3 voices; fols. 55ᵛ–56.

CONCORDANCES
Manuscript
St. Gall 463, no. 34; anon.; S only, with text.

Early Printed Collections
Antico 1520⁶, no. 12; anon.; *a 3*; text in S and B; T wanting.
Rhaw 1542⁸, no. 86; anon.; *a3*; text in all voices.
Berg and Neuber [1560]¹, no. 47; anon.; *a 3*; text in all voices.

Modern Editions
Bernstein, *Cantus Firmus in the French Chanson*, 2: 661; Mouton (after Rhaw 1542⁸).
Gaines, *Rhau:Tricinia*, 2:502; anon. (after Rhaw 1542⁸).

Intabulations
Brown, *Instrumental Music Printed before 1600*, lists the following collections: 1545₃, p. 53, no. 42; 1547₇, fol. F₄ᵛ, no. 33; 1555₂, fol. E₃ᵛ, no. 64; 1563₁₂, fol. 47, no. 100; 1564₇, fol. 26, no. 28; 1568₆, fol. 17, no. 37.

TYPE OF COMPOSITION
Chanson rustique based on an unknown popular monophonic melody.

RELATED COMPOSITION

The following composition is based on the same *cantus prius factus;* it is different from the London Add. 35087 setting.

Cambrai 125–128, fol. 146; anon.; *a 4;* text in all voices. Egenolff [c. 1535][14], I, no. 43; anon.; S only, with incipit "Jamais nemerai." Modern Edition: Maldeghem, *Trésor musical,* 18 (1882): 16, with text "Tout ce qui est au monde," and 19 (1883): 18, with text "Mon coeur couvert de sa gettes"; anon. (after Cambrai 125–128).

COMMENTARY TO THE TEXT

One stanza of text in each voice. Each portion of text underlaid in the repeated section (mm. 1–8) is discussed in its own paragraph below, followed by a third paragraph of commentary on mm. 9–20.

Mm. 2–3, Cambrai 125–128, St. Gall 463, Antico 1520[6], Berg and Neuber [1560][1], and Rhaw 1542[8] read either "masson" or "machon." M. 5, St. Gall 463, Antico 1520[6], Berg and Neuber [1560][1], and Rhaw 1542[8] have "ill." Mm. 5–6, S reads "barboulle," the present tense form; T and CT have "a barboulié," Rhaw 1542[8] has both "a barboullé" and "a bardouillé," and Berg and Neuber [1560][1] reads "a bardouillé." M. 6, S and T read "fron" (= front) in place of "con" (= cunt), as found in the other sources; CT has "que" for "con," probably in error. Mm. 7–8, T gives "sa troelle," and Cambrai 125–128 reads "cha trouelle."

Mm. 2–3, S has "mouton" (= sheep) for "bellin" (*bélier* = ram); T has "belin" in source and in Antico 1520[6], Berg and Neuber [1560][1], and Rhaw 1542[8]. M. 3, T has "q' " for "qu' "; CT has "que" for "qu' "; S and T read "aygno," for "agneau"; CT has "aigno" for "agneau," as found in the printed collections; Cambrai 125–128 inserts "ung" before "aigneau." Mm. 3–4, Antico 1520[6] and Rhaw 1542[8] have "que belle." M. 5, Cambrai 125–128 reads "seroy"; St. Gall 463 has "saurois"; and "sauroit" is found in Antico 1520[6], Berg and Neuber [1560][1], and Rhaw 1542[8]; and "sçauroit" is found in Antico 1520[6] and Rhaw 1542[8]. M. 6, S reads "fron" for "con"; T has "que" for "con"; CT lacks "con," as found in the other sources; S has "sy." Mm. 6–8, Cambrai 125–128 gives "si n'a la chandeille" and "si n'a chandeille"; Antico 1520[6] has "s'il n'a chandelle"; and Berg and Neuber [1560][1] reads "si n'a candelle."

M. 9, T has "nuit," as found in St. Gall 463 and Antico 1520[6]. M. 10, all sources except London Add. 35087 have "my," a variant of "me"; CT reads "dysoit." M. 12, T and CT read "nuysoit"; Cambrai 125–128 shows "l'empeschoit," meaning "stopped him (from performing)," for "luy nuysoyt." M. 13, source has "le" for "la," as found in the printed collections (*le* is a variant of *la* in Old French). Mm. 14–15, Cambrai 125–128 has "ruay" (hurled or cast aside violently) for "gesis" (*jetai* = threw). M. 17, T of source and Antico 1520[6] have "mays"; S has "enquore"; and CT reads "encquor."

COMMENTARY TO THE TRANSCRIPTION

M. 2, beat 3–m. 3, beat 1, CT, dotted half-note (f) in Antico 1520[6], Berg and Neuber [1560][1], and Rhaw 1542[8]. M. 3, S, note 2 is c" in St. Gall 463, Antico 1520[6], Berg and Neuber [1560][1], and Rhaw 1542[8]; CT, note 2 is a in Antico 1520[6], Berg and Neuber [1560][1], and Rhaw 1542[8]. M. 4, S reads quarter-note (b'-flat), two eighth-notes (a', g'), and whole-note (a') in St. Gall 463, Antico 1520[6], Berg and Neuber [1560][1], and Rhaw 1542[8], thus lengthening the phrase two beats; T, note 3 is whole-note (f') in Rhaw 1542[8], which lengthens the phrase two beats; CT, note 2 is whole-note, (f) in Antico 1520[6], Berg and Neuber [1560][1], and Rhaw 1542[8], which lengthens the phrase two beats. M. 5, T, notes 4 and 5 are quarter-notes in Rhaw 1542[8]. M. 7, beats 1–2, T, four eighth-notes (b-flat, a, g, f) in Rhaw 1542[8]; S, beats 2–3 are half-note (f') in Antico 1520[6], Berg and Neuber [1560][1], and Rhaw 1542[8], and two quarter-notes (f', f') in St. Gall 463.

Full repetitions of mm. 1–8 are written out in St. Gall 463, Antico 1520[6], Berg and Neuber [1560][1], and Rhaw 1542[8], with mm. 5–8 repeated again in St. Gall 463. M. 9, T, note 4 is b-flat in Rhaw 1542[8]; CT, note 4 is B-flat in Antico 1520[6], Berg and Neuber [1560][1], and Rhaw 1542[8]. M. 10, T, note 1 is g in Rhaw 1542[8]. M. 11, beats 1–2, S, two eighth-notes and quarter-note in Berg and Neuber [1560][1]; T, note 4 is b-flat in Rhaw 1542[8]; CT, note 4 is B-flat in Antico 1520[6], Berg and Neuber [1560][1], and Rhaw 1542[8]. M. 12, T, note 1 is g in Rhaw 1542[8]. M. 14, note 3–m. 15, quarter-rest, T, dotted half-note (c') in Rhaw 1542[8]; CT, dotted half-note (f) in Antico 1520[6], Berg and Neuber [1560][1], and Rhaw 1542[8]. M. 15, S, note 2 is c" in St. Gall 463, Antico 1520[6], Berg and Neuber [1560][1], and Rhaw 1542[8]; CT, note 2 is a in Antico 1520[6], Berg and Neuber [1560][1], and Rhaw 1542[8]. M. 16, S reads quarter-note (b'-flat), two eighth-notes (a', g'), and whole-note (a'), which lengthens the phrase two beats in St. Gall 463, Antico 1520[6], Berg and Neuber [1560)[1], and Rhaw 1542[8]; T, note 3 is a whole-note (f'), which lengthens the phrase two beats in Rhaw 1542[8]; CT, note 2 is a whole-note (f), which lengthens the phrase two beats in Antico 1520[6], Berg and Neuber [1560][1], and Rhaw 1542[8]. M. 17, T, notes 4 and 5 are quarter-notes in Rhaw 1542[8]. M. 19, beats 1–2, T, four eighth-notes (b-flat, a, g, f) in Rhaw 1542[8]; S, beats 2–3 are half-note (f') in St. Gall 463, Antico 1520[6], Berg and Neuber [1560][1], and Rhaw 1542[8]. Repetitions of mm. 17–20 are written out in Berg and Neuber [1560][1], Rhaw 1542[8], and in the S only of St. Gall 463 and Antico 1520[6]. M. 20, CT, note is e in Rhaw 1542[8], an obvious error.

[12] J'ayme bien mon amy

[Johannes Ghiselin] Verbonnet; 3 voices; fols. 44ᵛ–45.

CONCORDANCES
Modern Edition
Ghiselin, *Opera Omnia,* 4:13 (after London Add. 35087).

TYPE OF COMPOSITION
Chanson rustique based on a popular monophonic melody, one version of which appears in Paris 9346, fol. 29ᵛ (published in Gérold, *Manuscrit de Bayeux,* no. 29).

RELATED COMPOSITIONS
The following compositions are all based on the same *cantus prius factus;* they are all different from the London Add. 35087 setting and from each other.

1. Cambridge 1760, fol. 62ᵛ; N. le petit ("Fevin" given in table of contents); *a 3;* text in all voices.

2. Gardane 1542¹⁸, p. 23; Françoys du boys; *a 3;* text in all voices. Gardane 1543²¹, p. 24; Françoys du boys; *a 3;* text in all voices. Gardane 1559²¹, p. 24; Fransçois du bois; *a 3;* text in all voices. Scotto 1587⁸ (= Gardane 1543²¹), p. 19; Fransçoys du boys; *a 3;* text in all voices.

3. Antico 1520³, fol. 31ᵛ; anon.; *a 4;* two given voices with text form the antecedent parts of a double canon; the lower given voice carries the *cantus prius factus.*

4. Antico 1520³, fol. 35ᵛ; Adrien [Willaert]; *a 4;* two given voices with text form the antecedent parts of a double canon; both given voices have the *cantus prius factus.*

5. Antico 1520³, fol. 36ᵛ; Adrien [Willaert]; *a 4;* two given voices with text form the antecedent parts of a double canon; both given voices have the *cantus prius factus.*

Bernstein, *Cantus Firmus in the French Chanson,* 1: 403, states that "it is difficult to determine whether Verbonnet's chanson or that by Nino *[sic]* le Petit came first." Therefore, "either version could have served as model" for the other. Clytus Gottwald, *Johannes Ghiselin-Johannes Verbonnet. Stilkritische Untersuchung zum Problem ihrer Identität* (Wiesbaden: Breitkopf & Härtel, 1962), Anhang, pp. 14–15, provides a table of tenors from the Bayeux MS, Verbonnet, and Le Petit (which Gottwald attributes to Févin) settings and a reconstruction of the *cantus prius factus* based on these sources. Clinkscale, *Févin,* p. 197, attributes the Cambridge 1760 setting to Le Petit and suggests that the ascription to Févin in the table of contents was an error made by the scribe.

COMMENTARY TO THE TEXT
One stanza of text in each voice. Mm. 1–2, Paris 9346 reads "J'aymeray"; Gérold, *Manuscrit de Bayeax,* has "J'aimeray," meaning "I will love." M. 5, T and CT read "vray"; Cambridge 1760, Lotrian 1543, fo[...] Paris 9346, Antico 1520³, Gardane 1542¹⁸, Gard[...] 1543²¹, Gardane 1559²¹, and Scotto 1587⁸ have va[...] ants of "bon" for "vrais." Mm. 9–10, T and CT hav[...] "say." M. 10, S has "qui." M. 13, T and CT have "oussi"; Cambridge 1760 reads "aussy"; and Lotrian 1543, Paris 9346, Antico 1520³, Gardane 1542¹⁸, Gardane 1543²¹, Gardane 1559²¹, and Scotto 1587⁸ have "aussi." Mm. 14–17, Paris 9346, Antico 1520³, Gardane 1542¹⁸, Gardane 1543²¹, Gardane 1559²¹, and Scotto 1587⁸ read "fais je"; Lotrian 1543 has "faictz je."

Paris 9346 provides one extra stanza, and Lotrian 1543 supplies three (the first of which matches the extra stanza from Paris 9346) for this reading. Howard M. Brown, *Music in the French Secular Theater, 1400–1550* (Cambridge, Mass., 1963), p. 231, lists three other text sources: (1) *S'ensuyvent plusieurs belles chansons nouvelles avec plusieurs aultres retirées des anciennes impressions* (Paris, 1535), p. 155; (2) *S'ensuyvent plusieurs belles chansons nouvelles et fort joyeuses avec plusieurs autres retirées des anciennes impressions* (Paris, 1537), fol. 77; (3) Clément Marot, ed., *Les Chansons nouvellement assemblées oultre les anciennes impressions,* S.l. (1538), fol. 96. L. 2, Paris 9346 has "sçay" for "congnois" and adds "bien." L. 3, Paris 9346 gives "seroye." L. 8, "mais que" is equivalent to *pourvu que* (= provided that); "ayt" is equivalent to *ait.* L. 9, "pry" is equivalent to *prie.* L. 12, "obeyr" is equivalent to *obéir.*

COMMENTARY TO THE TRANSCRIPTION
No variants.

[13] Je my soloye aller esbatre

Anon.; 3 voices; fols. 90ᵛ–91.

CONCORDANCES
None.

TYPE OF COMPOSITION
Chanson rustique based on an unknown popular monophonic melody.

RELATED COMPOSITIONS
None.

COMMENTARY TO THE TEXT
One stanza of text in S; incomplete stanzas in T and CT. Mm. 1–10, CT reads "Je my soloye aller esbatre avecq" only. Mm. 1–5, "my" is the equivalent of "me." Mm. 9–12, "ches" is the equivalent of "ces." M. 10, "gen[ti]lz" is illegible in S. Mm. 9–15, the text "Avecq ches gen[ti]lz galans," appearing in the S, was editorially chosen over "Avecq mes petys enfans," appearing in source in T and in source and edition in mm. 20–31. M. 30, T has "sy." M. 32, T reads "me." Mm. 40–48, T lacks "Dieu les benysse!"

COMMENTARY TO THE TRANSCRIPTION
All emendations are made for the sake of the text

3–4, T, two quarter-notes (a, a).
...at 1, CT, dotted half-note (d).
'ted half-note (b-flat). M. 35,
...f-notes. M. 43, beats 1–3, CT,
...J. M. 44, beats 1–3, T, dotted half-

...ssiez parler, lessiez dire

Anon.; 3 voices; fols. 32ᵛ–33.

CONCORDANCES
None.

TYPE OF COMPOSITION
Chanson rustique based on an unknown popular monophonic melody.

RELATED COMPOSITIONS
The following compositions are based on another *cantus prius factus;* they are different from the London Add. 35087 setting and from each other, but parts of their texts are similar.

1. Munich 1508, no. 102; anon.; *a 6;* the first text line in all voices is the same as that in the London Add. 35087 text, but the remaining lines are different.

2. Attaingnant 1538¹⁰, no. 24; Mittantier; *a 4;* the final quatrain of *Amours si m'ont cousté cent livres* is the same text as London Add. 35087.

COMMENTARY TO THE TEXT
One stanza of text in each voice. Mm. 1–2, all voices read "Lessies." Mm. 3–4, S and CT give "lessies"; T has "lessis." M. 6, CT has "Lessies." Mm. 8–9, T and CT read "voldra." Mm. 15–17, S reads "J'aimeray quy m'aymera." Mm. 17–18, CT lacks "et" and has "j'aimeray quy." M. 20, S reads "quy."

COMMENTARY TO THE TRANSCRIPTION
No variants.

[15] Ma maistresse, m'amye

Anon.; 3 voices; fols. 22ᵛ–23.

CONCORDANCES
None.

TYPE OF COMPOSITION
Chanson rustique based on an unknown popular monophonic melody.

RELATED COMPOSITIONS
None.

COMMENTARY TO THE TEXT
One stanza of text in each voice. Mm. 2–3, T reads "maitresse." Mm. 6–7, S has "n'oublies"; CT gives "ne oublies." Mm. 14–16, S and T read "oublye."

COMMENTARY TO THE TRANSCRIPTION
M. 4, beat 4–m. 5, note 1, T, quarter-note (c') and eighth-note (c'); emendation made for the sake of the text.

[16] Mon mary m'a diffamée

[Josquin Desprez]; 3 voices; fols. 21ᵛ–22.

CONCORDANCES
Manuscripts
Brussels IV. 90—Tournai 94, no. 10; anon.; text in S (first four lines only) and T; CT music and text wanting.

Early Printed Collection
Le Roy and Ballard 1578¹⁵, fol. 16ᵛ; Josquin; *a 3,* text in all voices.

Modern Editions
Benthem, *Josquin's Three-part "Chansons rustiques,"* p. 444 (CT and text after London Add. 35087; S after Brussels IV. 90; T after Tournai 94).

Brown, *Early Music Series,* no. [EM]3; Josquin des Prez (after London Add. 35087).

Intabulation
Brown, *Instrumental Music Printed before 1600,* lists 1507₂, fol. 23ᵛ, no. 18.

TYPE OF COMPOSITION
Chanson rustique based on a popular monophonic melody, one version of which appears in Paris 12744, fol. 75 (published in Paris-Gevaert, *Chansons,* no. 111).

RELATED COMPOSITIONS
The following compositions are all based on the same *cantus prius factus;* they are all different from the London Add. 35087 setting and from each other.

1. Paris 1597, fol. 69ᵛ; anon.; *a 4;* text in all voices. Modern Edition: Shipp, *Chansonnier of Dukes of Lorraine,* p. 526; anon. (after Paris 1597).

2. Petrucci 1502², fol. 15ᵛ; De Orto; *a 4;* incipit "Mon mari ma deffamee" in S and T. Modern Edition: Hewitt, *Canti B,* p. 128; De Orto (after Petrucci 1502²).

3. Petrucci 1504³, fol. 44ᵛ; anon.; *a 4;* incipit "Mon mari ma defamee" in all voices.

4. Antico 1520³, fol. 37ᵛ; Adrien [Willaert]; *a 4;* two given voices with text form the antecedent parts for a double canon; both voices resemble the *cantus prius factus.*

COMMENTARY TO THE TEXT
One stanza of text in each voice. Each portion of text underlaid in the repeated section (mm. 1–18) is discussed in its own paragraph below, followed by a third paragraph of commentary on mm. 19–34. A fourth paragraph deals with the additional verses.

Mm. 9–18, Paris 1597 reads "et en despit de mon amy," and Le Roy and Ballard 1578¹⁵ gives "par despit de mon amy."

Mm. 1–5, Paris 12744 has "de" for "pour." Mm. 10–13, Paris 1597, Paris 12744, and Jeffery, *Chanson Verse* 90(a), no. 32, and 53, no. 20, give "faicte."

At the beginning of the refrain (m. 19), Paris 12744 gives "Hé! mon amy!," an extra line which does not fit the music of Josquin's setting in London Add. 35087 or Le Roy and Ballard 1578[15]; Tournai 94 and Antico 1520[3] omit this line also; however, Paris 1597 gives a different line, "Et mon amy, et mon amy," at this point, and Lotrian 1543, fol. 96, and Jeffery, *Chanson Verse* 90(a) and 53 give "O mon amy! O mon amy!" as an extra refrain line. Mm. 19–24, Paris 1597 reads "Et en despit de mon mari." Mm. 23–28, Paris 1597 gives "Qui m'y va ainsi batant"; Le Roy and Ballard 1578[15] has "Qui me va ainsi bastant." Mm. 28–32, S and T of source and Jeffery, *Chanson Verse* 90(a) and 53 read "j'en" for "je"; T has "pys," and Paris 1597 gives "pire."

Paris 12744 provides four additional stanzas for this reading, all with the extra refrain line "Hé! mon amy!" "Davant," which appears at the end of all but the second additional stanza of Paris 12744, has been changed here to "devant" to be consistent with London Add. 35087. Lotrian 1543 and Jeffery, *Chanson Verse* 90(a) and 53 contain two similar extra stanzas, both with the extra refrain line "O mon amy!" Lotrian 1543 and Jeffery, *Chanson Verse* 90(a) give abbreviated refrains, with Lotrian 1543 reading "O mon amy! / En despit de mon mary" only. Hewitt, *Canti B*, p. 38, discusses the Lotrian text. Jeffery, *Chanson Verse* 53 gives the full refrain. L. 1, "j'ay veu" precedes "quand j'estoi couchée" in Jeffery, *Chanson Verse* 53, meaning "I observed when I was in bed." L. 3, "si" precedes "fachée" in Jeffery, *Chanson Verse* 90(a) and 53. L. 10, Jeffrey, *Chanson Verse* 53 substitutes "courir" for "couchée," with change in meaning: "running around with my love."

COMMENTARY TO THE TRANSCRIPTION
    M. 9, CT, note is c' in Le Roy and Ballard 1578[15]. M. 10, S, notes 1 and 2 are quarter-notes in Le Roy and Ballard 1578[15]. M. 10, note 4–m. 11, note 2, S, half-note (e") in Le Roy and Ballard 1578[15]. M. 12, beats 1–2, S, quarter-note (d") and two eighth-notes (c", b') in Le Roy and Ballard 1578[15]. M. 12, note 4–m. 13, note 2, S, half-note (b') in Brussels IV.90 and Le Roy and Ballard 1578[15]. M. 16, note 2–m. 17, note 5, S, half-note (a') in Le Roy and Ballard 1578[15]. M. 16, beat 4–m. 17, beat 2, T, quarter-note (d'), four eighth-notes (c', b, a, g) in Tournai 94 and Le Roy and Ballard 1578[15]. M. 17, beats 3–4, T, two quarter-notes (a, a) in Le Roy and Ballard 1578[15]. M. 19, note 4–m. 20, note 2, CT, half-note (a') in Le Roy and Ballard 1578[15]. M. 21, CT, note 3 is b-flat in Le Roy and Ballard 1578[15]. M. 21, note 2–m. 22, note 2, S, two quarter-notes (d", e") in Brussels IV.90 and Le Roy and Ballard 1578[15]. M. 26, CT, note 1 is a quarter-note and note 2 is a half-note in Le Roy and Ballard 1578[15]. M. 28, note 5–m. 29, note 2, CT, half-note (a) in Le Roy and Ballard 1578[15]. M. 30, beats 1–4, T reads half-note (g) and half-rest in Tournai 94 and Le Roy and Ballard 1578[15]; CT, note 5 is a quarter-note, which has been emended here to read eighth-note af-

ter Le Roy and Ballard 1578[15]. M. 30, note 6–m. 31, note 2, CT, half-note (a') in Le Roy and Ballard 1578[15]. M. 32, beats 1–3, S, six eighth-notes (g', a', b', c", d", e") in Brussels IV.90 and Le Roy and Ballard 1578[15]; CT, beats 2–4 are six eighth-notes (g, a, b, c', d', b) in Le Roy and Ballard 1578[15].

[17] *N'est il point bien infortuné*

Anon.; 3 voices; fols. 30[v]–31.

CONCORDANCES
None.

TYPE OF COMPOSITION
Chanson rustique based on an unknown popular monophonic melody.

RELATED COMPOSITIONS
None.

COMMENTARY TO THE TEXT
    One stanza of text in each voice. M. 2, S reads "pas" instead of "point." Mm. 8–10, S has "leallement." Mm. 14–23, CT reads "a aultruy est habandonné."

COMMENTARY TO THE TRANSCRIPTION
No variants.

[18] *Nostre saison est bien fortunée*

Anon.; 3 voices; fols. 31[v]–32.

CONCORDANCES
None.

TYPE OF COMPOSITION
Chanson rustique based on an unknown popular monophonic melody.

RELATED COMPOSITIONS
None.

COMMENTARY TO THE TEXT
    One stanza of text in each voice. Mm. 3–4, S and CT read "et." Mm. 10–11, CT has "party." M. 11, "no" is an alternate form of "notre." Mm. 11–12, S has "mason." Mm. 14–15, S and T read "aler." Mm. 14–16, T gives "choucies"; S has "coucher." Mm. 17–18, T and CT have "buyson." Mm. 22–26, S reads "al la gellée." The literal translation of the text is nonsensical.

COMMENTARY TO THE TRANSCRIPTION
No variants.

[19] *Petite camusette*

[Antoine de Févin]; 3 voices; fols. 87[v]–88.

CONCORDANCES
Manuscripts
    Cambridge 1760, fol. 57[v]; Anth. de fevin; *a 3*; incipits "Petite camusette" in S and T and "Petitte camusette" in CT.

Munich 1516, no. 154; anon.; *a 3*; incipit "Petite camusete" in all voices.

Early Printed Collections
Formschneider 1538[9], no. 79; anon.; *a 3*; incipit "Petite camusette" in T.

Le Roy and Ballard 1578[16], fol. 23[v]; Iosquin (in T); *a 3*; text in all voices.

Modern Editions
Clinkscale, *Févin*, p. 479 (after Cambridge 1760).

Whisler, *Munich 1516*, 2:402; Févin (after Munich 1516).

Type of Composition
Chanson rustique based on an unknown popular monophonic melody.

Related Compositions
The following compositions are all based on the same *cantus prius factus;* they are all different from the London Add. 35087 setting and from each other.

1. Munich 1516, no. 134; anon.; *a 3*; incipits "Petit camusete" in S, "Petit camusette" in T, and "Pettit camusette" in CT. Modern Edition: Whisler, *Munich 1516*, 2:348; anon. (after Munich 1516).

2. Brussels 11239, fol. 20[v]; anon.; S and T only, with "Petite camusette" text ("Petite camusette" in T). Dijon 517, fol. 161[v]; anon.; *a 4*; "Selle mamera" *rondeau cinquain* text in S; "Petite camusette" text in other voices. Florence 2439, fol. 31[v]; Ockeghem; *a 4*; "Petite camusette" text in T and incipits "Petite camusette" in T and B and "Pettite camusette" in CT. Montecassino 871N, fol. 160[v]; anon.; *a 4*; incipit "Petite camusete" in S. Munich 1516, no. 11; anon.; *a 4*; incipit "Petite camusete" in all voices. New Haven, Mellon, fol. 4[v]; J. Okeghem; *a 4*; three lower voices have the "Petite camusette" text; S has text beginning "Petitte camusette, jay propose"; the remaining lines are similar to the *rondeau* refrain text. Paris, Nivelle de la Chaussée, fol. 55[v]; Okeghem; *a 4*; complete "Selle mamera" text in S; "Petite camusete" text in other voices. Seville 7–I–28, fol. 101[v], anon.; *a 4*; refrain stanza "De la momera" in S; incomplete "Petit le camiset" text in A and T; incipit "Petit le" in B. Wolfenbüttel 287, fol. 61[v]; anon.; *a 4*; complete "Selle maymera" text in S; "Petite camusette" text in other voices. Petrucci 1504[3], fol. 124[v]; Okenghem; *a 4*; incipit "Petite camusete" in all voices. Modern Editions: Gombosi, *Obrecht*, 2:8; Jan van Okeghem (after Petrucci 1504[3] and Florence 2439). Newton, *Florence 2439*, 2:93; Ockeghem (after Florence 2439). Picker, *Chanson Albums of Marguerite of Austria*, p. 437; Johannes Ockeghem (S and T after Brussels 11239; A and B after Petrucci 1504[3] with variants from other sources). Picker, *Chanson Albums of Marguerite*, 2:330; Johannes Ockeghem (after Brussels 11239, etc.). Pope and Kanazawa, *Montecassino 871*, p. 438; J. Ockeghem (after Montecassino 871N). Whisler, *Munich 1516*, 2:36; Ockeghem (after Munich 1516). Ock-

eghem's monotextual and bitextual chanson is discussed by Maria Rika Maniates, "Combinative Chansons in the Dijon Chansonnier," *Journal of the American Musicological Society* 23 (Summer 1970): 238f., and Picker, *Chanson Albums of Marguerite of Austria*, p. 81.

3. Antico 1520[3], fol. 22[v]; anon.; two given voices with text form the antecedent parts for a double canon; the lower voice carries the *cantus prius factus.*

4. Antico 1520[3], fol. 28[v]; Adrian [Willaert]; two given voices with text form the antecedent parts for a double canon; although both voices manipulate the popular melody, the lower part carries the true *cantus prius factus.*

5. Bologna R 142, fol. 32[v]; Iosquin; T only, with incipit "Pethite camuse." Leipzig 49—A: fol. 194, T: fol. 172[v], B: fol. 185; anon.; text "Petite et accipietis" in three extant voices; the direction "Fuga in epidiapente" given above T indicates the entry of the canonic voice. Rome P. L. 1980, 1981—*Quinta pars:* fol. 74, *Sexta pars:* fol. 78; anon.; incipits "Petitte camusete" in *Quinta pars* and "Petitte camusette" in *Sexta pars.* Susato 1545[15], no. 18; Iosquin de Pres; *a 6*; text in all voices. Attaingnant 1549, no. 19; Josquin des Pres (attribution in title); *a 6*; text in all voices. Modern Editions: Greenberg-Maynard, *Anthology of Early Renaissance Music*, p. 174; Josquin des Prez (after Susato 1545[15]). Josquin, *Wereldlijke Werken*, ser. 4, vol. 2:43 (after Bologna R 142, Susato 1545[15], and Attaingnant 1549). Smijers, *Van Ockeghem tot Sweelinck*, V, 158; Josquin des Prez (after Josquin, *Wereldlijke Werken*).

6. Kriesstein, 1540[7], no. 33; Adrianus VVillart; *a 6*; text in all voices; S–*Sexta pars* canon in refrain sections encompassed by freely imitative voices. Le Roy and Ballard 1572[2], fol. 57; Ad. Vuillard; *a 6*; text in all voices. Intabulation: Brown, *Instrumental Music before 1600*, lists 1547[5], fol. 47[v], no. 76.

7. Le Roy and Ballard 1572[2], fol. 75; Crequillon; *a 7*; text in all voices; this setting contains a triple canon.

Commentary to the Text
One stanza of text in each voice. Mm. 1–2, S reads "petitte." M. 25, at this point Susato 1545[15] and Attaingnant 1549 interpolate "S'en vont au bois joy[i]," meaning "Go into the pretty woods," and Antico 1520[3], fol. 22[v], and Antico 1520[3], fol. 28[v], interpolate "S'en vont au bois jouer," meaning "Go into the woods to play." Mm. 25–33, Antico 1520[3], fol. 22[v], and S of Le Roy and Ballard 1578[16] lack "Il s'en vont bras à bras." Mm. 30 and 33, CT and T read "et" for "il." Mm. 30–39, Antico 1520[3], fol. 22[v], lacks "Il s'en sont endormys." Mm. 31–35, Antico 1520[3], fol. 28[v], Attaingnant 1549, Le Roy and Ballard 1572[2], Le Roy and Ballard 1578[16], and Susato 1545[15] give "se" for "s'en." M. 39, T reads "petitte." Mm. 51–52, T has "m'avez."

Commentary to the Transcription
T has b-flat in signature, which does not appear in succeeding staves, in Cambrige 1760. M. 5, beats 1–4,

S, two half-notes (a′, a′) in Munich 1516 and Form-schneider 1538[9]. M. 6, beats 1–4, T, two half-notes (d′, d′) in Formschneider 1538[9]. M. 9, note 5–m. 10, note 2, T, half-note (e′) in Munich 1516 and Le Roy and Ballard 1578[16]. M. 10, beats 2–3, T, half-note (d′) in Cambridge 1760 and dotted quarter (d′), eighth-note (c′) in Le Roy and Ballard 1578[16]. M. 11, beat 2–m. 12, beat 2, T, dotted quarter-note (a), eighth-note (b), quarter-note (c′), dotted quarter-note (b), two sixteenth-notes (a, g) in Formschneider 1538[9]. M. 12, beats 1–4, CT, two half-notes (d, d) in Formschneider 1538[9]. M. 13, note 6–m. 14, note 2, T, half-note (b) in Munich 1516 and Le Roy and Ballard 1578[16]. M. 14, beats 1–2, S, half-note (e′) in Cambridge 1760, Munich 1516, and Le Roy and Ballard 1578[16]; S, note 1 is a dotted quarter-note and notes 2–3 are sixteenth-notes in Form-schneider 1538[9]. M. 18, beat 1, S, quarter-note (b′) in Le Roy and Ballard 1578[16]. M. 21, beat 1, T, two eighth-notes (e′, d′) in Cambridge 1760, Munich 1516, and Formschneider 1538[9]. M. 22, beat 1–m. 23, beat 2, S, dotted whole-note (f′); emended here for the sake of the text underlay after Cambridge 1760, Munich 1516, Formschneider 1538[9], and Le Roy and Ballard 1578[16]. M. 22, beat 4–m. 24, beat 4, T, four eighth-notes (a, g, a, b), five quarter-notes (c′, f, c′, c′, g), half-note (a) in Le Roy and Ballard 1578[16]. M. 24, beats 1–2, T, two quarter-notes (g, g) in Formschneider 1538[9]. M. 27, CT, notes 1 and 2 are lacking in Formschneider 1538[9]. M. 28, beat 1–m. 31, beat 4, S, double whole-note (a′), half-note (a′), dotted whole-note (a′) in Munich 1516; S, two double whole-notes (a′, a′) in Formschneider 1538[9]. M. 30, beat 1–m. 33, beat 4, CT, two double whole-notes (a, a) in Formschneider 1538[9]. M. 33, beat 1–m. 36, beat 4, T, two double whole-notes (e′, e′) in Formschneider 1538[9]. M. 34, S, note 1 is a′ in Form-schneider 1538[9]. M. 34, beat 1–m. 35, beat 4, T, two whole-notes (e′, e′) in Munich 1516. M. 35, beat 3–m. 36, beat 2, CT, whole-note (e) in Formschneider 1538[9], which fills the missing two beats in m. 27 of this source. M. 37, beat 3, S, two eighth-notes (b′, e) in Formschneider 1538[9]. M. 37, beat 4–m. 38, beat 1, S, dotted quarter-note (c″), two sixteenth-notes (b′, a′) in Cambridge 1760 and Le Roy and Ballard 1578[16]; T, two quarter-notes, emended here for the sake of the text underlay after Cambridge 1760, Munich 1516, Formschneider 1538[9], and Le Roy and Ballard 1578[16]. M. 38, beats 2–3, S, dotted quarter-note (a′), eighth-note (g′) in Formschneider 1538[9]. M. 39, beat 4–m. 40, beat 2, S, dotted quarter-note (g′), two eighth-notes (f′, f′), two sixteenth-notes (e′, d′) in Cambridge 1760, Munich 1516, and Formschneider 1538[9], and dotted quarter-note (g′), quarter-note (f′), two sixteenth-notes (e′, d′) in Le Roy and Ballard 1578[16]. M. 40, T, note 2 is a in Le Roy and Ballard 1578[16], and beats 3–4 are two quarter-notes (c′, c′) in Munich 1516. M. 40, last note–m. 41, note 2, S, half-note (a′) in Le Roy and Ballard 1578[16]. M. 41, beats 1–2, T, dotted quarter-

note (b), two sixteenth-notes (a, g) in Cambridge 1760, and beat 2 is two eighth-notes (a, g) in Le Roy and Ballard 1578[16]. M. 44, beat 4–m. 45, beat 2, S, dotted quarter-note (a′), two eighth-notes (g′, a′), two sixteenth-notes (g′, f′) in Munich 1516. M. 46, beat 4–m. 47, beat 1, S, two quarter-notes in Munich 1516. M. 46, beat 4–m. 47, beat 2, S, two eighth-notes (a′, g′), dotted quarter-note (a′), two sixteenth-notes (g′, f′) in Formschneider 1538[9] . M. 49, last note–m. 50, note 3, S, half-note (c″), two eighth-notes (b′, a′) in Cam-bridge 1760. M. 51, S, note 4 is d″ in Cambridge 1760 and Munich 1516, and beat 3 is quarter-note (e″) in Le Roy and Ballard 1578[16]. M. 51, note 2–m. 52, note 3, T, quarter-note (e′), dotted quarter-note (c′), eighth-note (d′), two quarter-notes (e′, f′) in Le Roy and Ballard 1578[16]. M. 51, beat 4–m. 52, beat 1, S, dotted quarter-note (f′), eighth-note (e″) in Formschneider 1538[9]. M. 52, beats 1–4, S, two eighth-notes (e″, d″), dotted quarter-note (d″), two eighth-notes (c″, c″), two sixteenth-notes (b′, c″) in Munich 1516; CT, whole-note (a) in Cambridge 1760.

[20] *Quant je vous voy parmy les rues*

Anon.; 3 voices; fols. 66ᵛ–68.

CONCORDANCES
None.

TYPE OF COMPOSITION
Chanson rustique based on an unknown popular monophonic melody.

RELATED COMPOSITIONS
None.

COMMENTARY TO THE TEXT
One stanza of text in each voice. Mm. 9–11, CT reads "ruez"; CT contains a repetition of "Quant je vous voy parmy les rues" under mm. 11–14, which would have delayed the underlaying of "Je vous souhaide toute nue" until mm. 14–18 and "Entre mes bras dessus mon lyt" until mm. 19–24 in the edition: this repetition has been omitted, and the second text line moved to provide the obvious textual-imitative musical relationship appearing among all voices in mm. 11–14 of the edition. M. 12, CT has "souhayde." M. 15, CT reads "me praes." Mm. 19–20, S and T have "braes." Mm. 28–31, T and CT give "caly."

COMMENTARY TO THE TRANSCRIPTION
No variants.

[21] *Que n'est il vray ma joye*

Anon.; 3 voices; fols. 68ᵛ–69.

CONCORDANCES
None.

TYPE OF COMPOSITION
Chanson rustique based on an unknown popular monophonic melody.

RELATED COMPOSITIONS
None.

COMMENTARY TO THE TEXT
Incomplete stanza (first two lines) in each voice. Mm. 13–17, CT adds "et" before "esperanche."

COMMENTARY TO THE TRANSCRIPTION
No variants.

[22] Qui est celuy qui dira mal du con

Anon.; 3 voices; fols. 42ᵛ–43.

CONCORDANCES
None.

TYPE OF COMPOSITION
Chanson rustique based on an unknown popular monophonic melody.

RELATED COMPOSITIONS
The following compositions are based on another *cantus prius factus;* they are similar to each other but different from the London Add. 35087 setting. Their texts, however, are related.
1. Antico 1536[1], no. 10; Adrien VVillaert; *a 3;* text in all voices. Petreius 1541[2], no. 85; Adrian VVillart; *a 3;* text in all voices. Le Roy and Ballard 1560, fol. 14ᵛ; Adrian VVillart; *a 3;* text in all voices. Scotto 1562[9], p. 12; Adrien Vuillaer; *a 3;* text in S and T; CT wanting. Le Roy and Ballard 1578[16], no. 3; Ad. Vuillard; *a 3;* text in all voices.
2. Antico 1536[1], no. 38; Richafort; *a 3;* text in all voices.

COMMENTARY TO THE TEXT
One stanza of text in each voice. Mm. 2–3, Antico 1536[1], nos. 10 and 38, Le Roy and Ballard 1560, Le Roy and Ballard 1578[16], Petreius 1541[2], and Scotto 1562[9] give the past tense form, "a dit," for "dira." M. 5, S and T read "fons" (= hollow vessel, expressing a similar idea as "con"), whereas CT of source, Le Roy and Ballard 1560, and Le Roy and Ballard 1578[16] have "non" for "con"; all other sources give "con." Mm. 6–7, all sources lack "celuy" except London Add. 35087. M. 9, all voices read "point" for "pas" and are amended after all other sources. Mm. 9–11, all voices have "gentilhoms." Mm. 11–12, all other sources have "le" for "tout." Mm. 14–17, all other sources have "la joye." Mm. 16–18, all sources lack "pourtant qu' " except London Add. 35087.

COMMENTARY TO THE TRANSCRIPTION
No variants.

[23] Si j'ayme mon amy

Anon.; 3 voices; fols. 24ᵛ–25.

CONCORDANCES
Manuscript

London Harley 5242, fol. 22ᵛ; anon.; S only, with nine stanzas of text.

TYPE OF COMPOSITION
Chanson rustique based on a popular monophonic melody, one version of which appears in Paris 12744, fol. 80ᵛ (published in Paris-Gevaert, *Chansons,* no. 118).

RELATED COMPOSITIONS
The following compositions are based on another *cantus prius factus;* they are different from the London Add. 35087 setting and from each other, but their texts are similar.
1. Florence 117, fol. 68ᵛ; anon.; *a 4;* text in all voices.
2. St. Gall 462, fol. 45; anon.; *a 3;* text in S and T (first three lines only) with four other stanzas given also; incipit "In minem sinn" placed above S. Modern Edition: Geering-Trümpy, *Liederbuch des Heer,* p. 87; anon. (after St. Gall 462).

COMMENTARY TO THE TEXT
One stanza of text in each voice. M. 1, Jeffery, *Chanson Verse* 90(a), no. 36, and 53, no. 36, have "se." M. 3, S has "mieux" for "plus," and St. Gall 462 and Jeffery, *Chanson Verse* 90(a) and 53 read "mieulx." Mm. 4–8, St. Gall 462 reads "Ce ne pas de merveille," Jeffery, *Chanson Verse* 90(a) and 53 have "Ce n'est pas de merveilles," and CT reads "mervielle." M. 10, St. Gall 462 reads "en" for "de," and all other sources have "ce" for "che." Mm. 12–15, all sources except London Add. 35087 read "que l'on fait" for "qui se faict," with no change in meaning, and CT gives "chandelle."

London Harley 5242 provides eight additional stanzas for this reading. Four similar or dissimilar stanzas appear in Paris 12744, St. Gall 462, and Jeffery, *Chanson Verse* 90(a), no. 36, and 53, no. 36. Ll. 5, 45, and 47, the "coquart" (= cuckolded husband) calls his wife "coquarde" (= saucy) and her friend "coquart" (= cocky), a very ironic play on words. L. 2, Paris 12744 gives "Lombard" for "vieillart" (the Lombards had a bad reputation during the Renaissance); Paris-Gevaert, *Chansons,* St. Gall 462; and Jeffery, *Chanson Verse* 90(a) and 53 substitute "fetard" (= slipshod) for "vieillart"; Geering-Trümpy, *Liederbuch des Heer,* mistakenly reads "fotard" in St. Gall 462; and St. Gall 462 also inserts "est" before "fetard," which ruins the meter. L. 4, St. Gall 462 has "coquart" for "paillart"; Jeffery, *Chanson Verse* 90(a) and 53 give "quoquart." L. 5, Paris 12744 reads "couart" (coward) for "coquart"; St. Gall 462, Jeffery, *Chanson Verse* 90(a) and 53, and Paris-Gevaert, *Chansons* substitute "vieillart" for "coquart." Ll. 7–8, Paris-Gevaert, *Chansons* gives "Quant suys avecques luy / Je n'ay que tout ennuy." Ll. 7–12, St. Gall 462 and Jeffery, *Chanson Verse* 90(a) and 53 have a different stanza here, "Si[e] je prens mon plaisir . . . Aux despens de sa bource!" L. 9, Paris 12744 reads "home" (= man) for "chose," as is also found in Paris-

Gevaert, *Chansons*. L. 10, Paris 12744 and Paris-Gevaert, *Chansons* give "Or feust ensevely." L. 13, "o" is the equivalent of "avec"; Paris 12744 and Paris-Gevaert, *Chansons* have "Et quant j'ay mon amy." Ll. 13–14, St. Gall 462 and Jeffery, *Chanson Verse* 90(a) and 53 read "Quant je suis avec luy / Je n'ay que tout ennuy," meaning "When I'm with him / I have nothing but torment." L. 14, the context makes it clear that "couché" should be feminine; Paris 12744 has "Couché aupres de mon amy"; Paris-Gevaert, *Chansons* has "Couché aupres de my," meaning "Sleeping next to me." L. 16, St. Gall 462 and Jeffery, *Chanson Verse* 90(a) and 53 read "S' il fust ense[p]vely" (similar to l. 10 of London Harley 5242). L. 17, "n'a il pas" is not clear in source (London Harley 5242); Paris 12744 has "Ne de jour ne de nuyt," meaning "In the daytime or at night." St. Gall 462 and Jeffery, *Chanson Verse* 90(a) and 53 have "Et en terre pourry" (same as London Harley 5242, l. 11). L. 18, Paris 12744 reads "suis" for "fuz"; St. Gall 462 and Jeffery, *Chanson Verse* 90(a) and 53 give "Je seroye à mon ay[i]se," and Geering-Trümpy, *Liederbuch des Heer* mistakenly reads "sy seroye" for "je seroye" in St. Gall 462. Ll. 19–24, Paris 12744 and Paris-Gevaert, *Chansons* give a different stanza, "Sy je fais mon desduit . . . Aux despens de sa bource!" (similar to ll. 7–12, St. Gall 462 and Jeffery, *Chanson Verse* 90(a) and 53). L. 19, St. Gall 462 and Jeffery, *Chanson Verse* 90(a) and 53 read "Quant je tiens mon amy," meaning "When I hold my friend [in my arms]." L. 20, St. Gall 462 and Jeffery, *Chanson Verse* 90(a) and 53 give "Couché avecque my," meaning "Sleeping with me" (similar to London Harley, l. 14). L. 21, St. Gall 462 and Jeffery, *Chanson Verse* 90(a) and 53 have "Il me tient embrassée" (same as London Harley 5242, l. 15), and Geering-Trümpy, *Liederbuch des Heer* mistakenly reads "ambrassée" for "embrassée." L. 22, St. Gall 462, Paris-Gevaert, *Chansons,* and Jeffery, *Chanson Verse* 90(a) and 53 read "Aussi fais je moy luy," meaning "And I do the same for him." L. 23, St. Gall 462 and Jeffery, *Chanson Verse* 90(a) and 53 give "D'avoir ung tel deduyt," meaning "Having such pleasure."

COMMENTARY TO THE TRANSCRIPTION

All variants listed here are those between London Add. 35087 and the S of London Harley 5242; there are no variants between the edition and London Add. 35087. M. 5, beat 3–m. 6, beat 1, six eighth-notes (e', f', g', f', g', f'). M. 6, beat 4–m. 7, beat 1, half-note (f'). M. 11, beat 3–end, seven quarter-notes (c', f', f', f', e', e', d'), two eighth-notes (c', b), quarter-note (a), half-note (d'), quarter note (c'), half-note (d'), quarter-rest, six quarter-notes (f', f', f', e', e', d'), two eighth-notes (c', b), quarter-note (a), half-note (d'), quarter-note (c'), double whole-note (d'), thus adding extra mm. in London Harley 5242.

[24] *Tout plain d'ennuy et de desconfort*

[Benedictus Appenzeller]; 3 voices; fols. 49v–51.

Concordances
Early Printed Collections
Susato [1552][11], no. 23; Benedictus; *a 3*; B only, with text.
Berg and Neuber 1560[2], no. 36; Benedictus, *a 3*; text in all voices.

Modern Editions
Adams, *Three-Part Chanson*, 2:633; Appenzeller (after London Add. 35087).
Thompson, *Appenzeller*, Appendix 1, p. 299 (after London Add. 35087).

Type of Composition
Chanson musicale.

Related Compositions
None.

Commentary to the Text
One stanza of text in each voice. Mm. 14–15, T reads "suy." Mm. 15–16, CT has "suys." Mm. 23–24, CT reads "port." Mm. 24–28, T has "port." Mm. 28–51, Berg and Neuber 1560[2] and Susato [1552][11] give "Seul regrettant celle à qui j'ay trop / Mis mon cueur et aultre mis en oublie."

Commentary to the Transcription
M. 11, S, note 5 is missing in Berg and Neuber 1560[2]. M. 36, beat 4–m. 37, beat 1, CT, quarter-note and two eighth-notes; emended for the sake of the text underlay after Susato [1552][11] and Berg and Neuber 1560[2]. M. 45, beats 1–4, S, half-note (g') and half-rest in Berg and Neuber 1560[2].

Appendix A: Sources

Abbreviations of sources are arranged alphabetically according to cities, libraries, and numbers for manuscripts; publishers and available RISM numbers for prints; and authors and editors for modern editions. Each *siglum* is followed by the full title of the source.

Manuscripts

Bologna Q 16	Bologna, Civico Museo Bibliografico Musicale, MS Q 16.
Bologna Q 17	Bologna, Civico Museo Bibliografico Musicale, MS Q 17.
Bologna Q 18	Bologna, Civico Museo Bibliografico Musicale, MS Q 18.
Bologna R 142	Bologna, Civico Museo Bibliografico Musicale, MS R 142.
Brussels 228	Brussels, Bibliothèque Royale de Belgique, MS 228.
Brussels 11239	Brussels, Bibliothèque Royale de Belgique, MS 11239.
Brussels IV.90	Brussels, Bibliothèque Royale de Belgique, MS IV.90 (cf. Tournai 94).
Cambrai 125–128	Cambrai, Bibliothèque Municipale, MSS 125–128.
Cambridge 1760	Cambridge, Magdalene College, MS Pepys 1760.
Copenhagen 1848	Copenhagen, Kongelige Bibliotek Ny Kgl. Samling, MS 1848–2°.
Dijon 517	Dijon, Bibliothèque de la Ville, MS 517.
Florence 107bis	Florence, Biblioteca Nazionale Centrale, MS Magl. XIX.107bis.
Florence 117	Florence, Biblioteca Nazionale Centrale, MS Magl. XIX.117.
Florence 121	Florence, Biblioteca Nazionale Centrale, MS Magl. XIX.121.
Florence 164–167	Florence, Biblioteca Nazionale Centrale, MS Magl. XIX.164–167.
Florence 178	Florence, Biblioteca Nazionale Centrale, MS Magl. XIX.178.
Florence 229	Florence, Biblioteca Nazionale Centrale, MS Banco Rari 229.
Florence 2356	Florence, Biblioteca Riccardiana, MS 2356.
Florence 2439	Florence, Biblioteca del Conservatorio di Musica, MS Basevi 2439.
Florence 2442	Florence, Biblioteca del Conservatorio di Musica, MS Basevi 2442.
Florence II.I. 232	Florence, Biblioteca Nazionale Centrale, MS II.I.232.
Heilbronn X. 2	Heilbronn, Gymnasialbibliothek, MS X. 2.
Leipzig 49	Leipzig, Bibliothek der Thomaskirche, MS 49 III A 19.
London Add. 19583	London, British Library, MS Add. 19583.
London Add. 29381	London, British Library, MS Add. 29381.
London Add. 31922	London, British Library, MS Add. 31922.
London Add. 35087	London, British Library, MS Add. 35087.
London Harley 5242	London, British Library, MS Harley 5242.
London Royal 20 A XVI	London, British Library, MS Royal 20 A XVI.
Modena α F.2.29	Modena, Biblioteca Estense, MS α F.2.29 (*olim* Lat. 782).
Montecassino 871N	Montecassino, Archivo della Badia, Cod. 871N.
Munich 1503a	Munich, Bayerische Staatsbibliothek, Mus. MS 1503a.
Munich 1508	Munich, Bayerische Staatsbibliothek, Mus. MS 1508.
Munich 1516	Munich, Bayerische Staatsbibliothek, Mus. MS 1516.
New Haven, Mellon	New Haven, Connecticut, Yale University, Library of the School of Music, Mellon Chansonnier.
Paris 1274	Paris, Bibliothèque Nationale, MS nouv. acq. fr. 1274 (de Vire MS).
Paris 1597	Paris, Bibliothèque Nationale, MS fonds fr. 1597.
Paris 2245	Paris, Bibliothèque Nationale, MS fonds fr. 2245.
Paris 4379	Paris, Bibliothèque Nationale, MS nouv. acq. fr. 4379 (manuscript fragments combined with Seville 5–I–43 to form a complete collection).

Paris 9346	Paris, Bibliothèque Nationale, MS fonds fr. 9346 (Bayeux MS).
Paris 12744	Paris, Bibliothèque Nationale, MS fonds fr. 12744.
Paris Vm[7] 676	Paris, Bibliothèque Nationale, Département de Musique, Res. Vm[7] 676.
Paris, Nivelle de la Chaussée	Paris (Neuilly-sur-Seine), Bibliothèque G. Thibault de Chambure, Nivelle de la Chaussée Chansonnier.
Perugia 431	Perugia, Biblioteca Comunale, Cod. 431.
Rome 2856	Rome, Biblioteca Casanatense, MS 2856.
Rome C. G. XIII.27	Vatican City, Biblioteca Apostolica Vaticana, Cappella Giulia, MS XIII.27.
Rome P. L. 1980, 1981	Vatican City, Biblioteca Apostolica Vaticana, MSS Palatini Latini 1980, 1981.
St. Gall 461	St. Gall, Stiftsbibliothek, Cod. 461 (Sicher Liederbuch).
St. Gall 462	St. Gall, Stiftsbibliothek, Cod. 462 (Heer Liederbuch).
St. Gall 463	St. Gall, Stiftsbibliothek, Cod. 463 (Tschudi Liederbuch).
Segovia	Segovia, Catedral, Archivo, MS.
Seville 5–I–43	Seville, Biblioteca Colombina, MS 5–I–43 (manuscript fragment combined with Paris 4379 to form a complete collection).
Seville 7–I–28	Seville, Biblioteca Colombina, MS 7–I–28.
Tournai 94	Tournai, Bibliothèque de la Ville, MS 94 (matching tenor partbook to Brussels IV.90 superius partbook).
Ulm 237[a–d]	Ulm, Bibliothek des Münsters, Schermar'sche Sammlung, MSS 237[a–d].
Uppsala 76a	Uppsala, Universitetsbiblioteket, Vokalmusik i handskrift, MS 76a.
Verona DCCLVII	Verona, Biblioteca Capitolare, Cod. DCCLVII.
Vienna 18746	Vienna, Österreichische Nationalbibliothek, Cod. 18746.
Washington, Laborde	Washington, D.C., Library of Congress, MS M.2.I.L25 Case (Laborde Chansonnier).
Wolfenbüttel 287	Wolfenbüttel, Landesbibliothek, MS extravag. 287.
Zwickau 78.3	Zwickau, Ratsschulbibliothek, MS 78.3.

Early Printed Collections

Antico 1520[2]	*Motetti novi libro tertio.* Venice, A. Antico, 1520.
Antico 1520[3]	*Motetti novi e chanzoni franciose a quatro sopra doi.* Venice, A. Antico, 1520.
Antico 1520[6]	*Chansons à troys.* Venice, A. Antico, L. A. Giunta, 1520.
Antico 1536[1]	*La courone et fleur des chansons à troys.* Venice, A. Antico (A. dell'Abbate), 1536.
Attaingnant 1529[4]	*Quarante et deux chansons musicales à troys parties nouvellement et correctement imprimées.* Paris, P. Attaingnant, 1529.
Attaingnant 1538[10]	*Premier livre contenant XXV chansons nouvelles a quatre parties en ung volume et en deux. . . .* Paris, P. Attaingnant et H. Jullet, 1538.
Attaingnant 1540[2]	*Missarum musicalium quatuor vocum cum suis motetis. Liber tertius.* Paris, P. Attaingnant et H. Jullet, 1540.
Attaingnant 1549	*Trente sixiesme livre contenant XXX chansons tres musicales, a quatre cinq et six parties, en cinq livres, dont le cinquiesme livre contient les cinquiesmes & sixiesmes parties, le tout de la composition de feu Josquin des Pres.* Paris, P. Attaingnant, 1549.
Berg and Neuber [1560][1]	*Selectissimorum triciniorum.* Nuremberg, J. von Berg & U. Neuber (s.d.).
Berg and Neuber 1560[2]	*Variarum linguarum tricinia, a praestantissimis musicis, ad voces fere aequales composita. . . . Tomi secundi.* Nuremberg, J. von Berg & U. Neuber, 1560.
Egenolff [c. 1535][14]	*[Lieder zu 3 & 4 Stimmen].* [Frankfurt a. M., C. Egenolff] (s.d.).
Formschneider 1538[9]	*Trium vocum carmina a diversis musicis composita.* Nuremberg, H. Formschneider, 1538.
Gardane 1541[13]	*Di Constantio Festa il primo libro di madrigali a tre voci, con la gionta de quaranta madrigali di Ihan Gero, novamente ristampato, et da molti errori emendato, aggiuntovi similmente trenta canzoni francese di Janequin.* Venice, A. Gardane, 1541.
Gardane 1542[18]	*Primo libro di madrigali d'Archadelt a tre voci, insieme alcuni di Const. Festa. Con la gionta di dodese canzoni francese et sei motteti novissimi.* Venice, A. Gardane, 1542.
Gardane 1543[21]	*Primo libro di madrigali d'Archadelt a tre voci con la gionta di dodese canzoni franzese et sei motteti novissimi.* Venice, A. Gardane, 1543.
Gardane 1543[23]	*Quaranta madrigali di Jhan Gero insieme trenta canzoni francese di Clement Janequin di nuovo ristampati a tre voci.* Venice, A. Gardane, 1543.

Gardane 1559[21]	*Il primo libro di madrigali d'Archadelt a tre voci, con la gionta di dodese canzon francese & sei motetti novissimi. Novamente ristampati.* Venice, A. Gardano, 1559.
Glareanus 1547[1]	Glareani ΔΩΔΕΚΑΧΟΡΔΟΝ. Basel, H. Petrus, 1547.
Kriesstein 1540[7]	*Selectissimae necnon familiarissimae cantiones, ultra centum vario idiomate vocum, tam multiplicium quam etiam paucar. Fugae quoque, ut vocantur. Besonder ausserlessner kunstlicher lustiger Gesang mancherlay Sprachen . . . von acht Stymmen an bis auf zwo: . . . sinngen und auf Instrument zubrauchen.* Augsburg, M. Kriesstein, 1540.
Le Roy and Ballard 1553[22]	*Tiers livre de chansons, composées a trois parties par bons et excellents musiciens, imprimées en un volume.* Paris, A. le Roy et R. Ballard, 1553.
Le Roy and Ballard 1560	*Cincquiesme livre de chansons composé a troys parties par M. Adrian Vuillart nouvellement.* Paris, A. le Roy et R. Ballard, 1560.
Le Roy and Ballard 1572[2]	*Mellange de chansons tant des vieux autheurs que des modernes, a cinq, six, sept, et huict parties.* Paris, A. le Roy et R. Ballard, 1572.
Le Roy and Ballard 1578[15]	*Second livre de chansons a trois parties composé par plusieurs autheurs.* Paris, A. le Roy et R. Ballard, 1578.
Le Roy and Ballard 1578[16]	*Tiers livre de chansons a trois parties composé par Ad. Vuillart.* Paris, A. le Roy et R. Ballard, 1578.
Lotrian 1543	*Sensuyt plusieurs belles chansons nouvelles et fort joyeuses avecques plusieurs aultres retirées des anciennes impressions comme pourrez veoir en la table en laquelle sont comprinses les premieres lignes des chansons.* Paris, A. Lotrian, 1543.
Petreius 1541[2]	*Trium vocum cantiones centum, à praestantissimis diversarum nationum ac linguarum musicis compositae. Tomi primi.* Nuremberg, J. Petreius, 1541.
Petrucci 1501	*Harmonice musices Odhecaton A.* Venice, O. Petrucci, 1501.
Petrucci 1502[2]	*Canti B. numero cinquanta B.* Venice, O. Petrucci, 1502.
Petrucci 1504[3]	*Canti C. N⁰ cento cinquanta.* Venice, O. Petrucci, 1504.
Rhaw 1542[8]	*Tricinia. Tum veterum tum recentiorum in arte musica symphonistarum, latina, germanica, brabantica & gallica, ante hac typis nunquam excusa, observato in disponendo tonorum ordine, quo utentibus sint accomodatiora.* Wittenberg, G. Rhaw, 1542.
Scotto 1562[9]	*Il terzo libro delle muse a tre voci. Di Canzon francese di Adrian Willaert nuovamente con alcune d'altri autori insieme ristampate et con somma diligenza corrette.* Venice, G. Scotto, 1562.
Scotto 1587[8]	*Di Archadelt il primo libro de madrigali motetti et canzoni francese a tre voci, novamente ristampati.* Venice, G. Scotto, 1587.
Susato 1545[14]	*Le sixiesme livre contenant trente et une chansons nouvelles a cincq et a six parties convenables et propices a jouer de tous instrumentz nouvellement imprimés . . .* Antwerp, T. Susato, 1545.
Susato 1545[15]	*Le septiesme livre contenant vingt et quatre chansons a cincq et a six parties, composées par feu de bonne memoire et tres excellent en musicque Josquin des Pres, avecq troix epitaphes dudict Josquin, composez par divers aucteurs . . .* Antwerp, T. Susato, 1545.
Susato [1552][11]	*La fleur de chansons et sixiesme livre à troix parties, contenant XXIII nouvelles chansons, propices a tous instrumentz musicaulx, composées par plusieurs bons maistres musiciens, . . .* Antwerp, T. Susato (s.d.).

Modern Editions

Adams, *Aspects of the Chanson*	Adams, Courtney S. "Some Aspects of the Chanson for Three Voices during the Sixteenth Century." *Acta musicologica* 49 (1977): 227–50.
Adams, *Three-Part Chanson*	Adams, Courtney S. "The Three-Part Chanson during the Sixteenth Century: Changes in Its Style and Importance." Ph.D. diss., University of Pennsylvania, 1974.
Agricola: *Opera Omnia*	*Alexandri Agricola: Opera omnia.* Edited by Edward R. Lerner. 5 vols. [Rome]: American Institute of Musicology, 1961–70.
Atlas, *The Cappella Giulia Chansonnier*	Atlas, Alan. *The Cappella Giulia Chansonnier (Rome, Biblioteca Apostolica Vaticana C.G. XIII, 27).* Brooklyn: Institute of Medieval Music, 1976.

Benthem, *Josquin's Three-part "Chansons rustiques"*

Benthem, Jaap van. "Josquin's Three-part 'Chansons rustiques': A Critique of the Readings in Manuscripts and Prints." *Josquin des Prez: Proceedings of the International Josquin Festival-Conference Held at the Julliard School, Lincoln Center, New York City, June, 1971.* London: Oxford University Press, 1976.

Bernoulli, *Aus Liederbüchern der Humanistenzeit*

Bernoulli, Eduard. *Aus Liederbüchern der Humanistenzeit: Eine bibliographische und notentypographische Studie.* Leipzig: Breitkopf & Härtel, 1910.

Bernstein, *Cantus Firmus in the French Chanson*

Bernstein, Lawrence F. "Cantus Firmus in the French Chanson for Two and Three Voices, 1500–1550." Ph.D. diss., New York University, 1969.

Besseler, *Die Musik des Mittelalters und der Renaissance*

Besseler, Heinrich, ed. *Die Musik des Mittelalters und der Renaissance.* Vol. 2 of *Handbuch der Musikwissenschaft,* edited by Ernst Büchen. 10 vols. Potsdam: Akademische Verlagsgesellschaft Athenaion, 1931.

Birmingham, *Chansonnier of Duke of Orleans*

Birmingham, Hugh M. "A Transcription into Modern Notation of a Chansonnier (Fonds Français 2245) of the Duke of Orleans, with Commentary and Concordance." Master's thesis, North Texas State University, 1955.

Blume, *Das Chorwerk*

Blume, Friedrich. *Josquin des Pres und andere Meister, Weltliche Lieder zu 3–5 Stimmen.* Vol. 3 of *Das Chorwerk,* edited by Friedrich Blume. 99 vols. Wolfenbüttel: Möseler Verlag, 1929–63.

Boer, *Chansonvormen*

Boer, Coenraad L. *Chansonvormen op het Einde van de XVde Eeuw: Een Studie naar Aanleiding van Petrucci's "Harmonice musices Odhecaton."* Amsterdam: H. J. Paris, 1938.

Brown, *Early Music Series*

Brown, Howard M. *Early Music Series.* No. [EM]3. London: Oxford University Press, 1973.

Brown, *Instrumental Music Printed before 1600*

Brown, Howard M. *Instrumental Music Printed before 1600.* Cambridge, Mass.: Harvard University Press, 1965.

Brown, *Parisian Chanson*

Brown, Howard M. "The Genesis of a Style: The Parisian Chanson, 1500–1530." In *Chanson & Madrigal 1480–1530, Studies in Comparison and Contrast,* edited by James Haar. Cambridge, Mass.: Harvard University Press, 1964.

Brown, *Theatrical Chansons*

Brown, Howard M. *Theatrical Chansons of the Fifteenth and Early Sixteenth Centuries.* Cambridge, Mass.: Harvard University Press, 1963.

Brumel: *Opera Omnia*

Antonii Brumel: Opera omnia. Edited by Barton Hudson. 6 vols. [Rome]: American Institute of Musicology, 1951–72.

Bukofzer, *Studies in Medieval and Renaissance Music*

Bukofzer, Manfred F. *Studies in Medieval and Renaissance Music.* New York: W. W. Norton, 1950.

Chaillon, *Le Chansonnier de Françoise*

Chaillon, Paule. "Le Chansonnier de Françoise (M. S. Harley 5242, Br. Mus.)." *Revue de musicologie* 35 (1953): 1–22.

Clinkscale, *Févin*

Clinkscale, Edward H. "The Complete Works of Antoine de Févin." Ph.D. diss., New York University, 1965.

Compère: *Opera Omnia*

Loyset Compère: Opera omnia. Edited by Ludwig Finscher. 5 vols. to date. [Rome]: American Institute of Musicology, 1958—.

Davison-Apel, *Historical Anthology of Music*

Davison, Archibald T., and Willi Apel. *Oriental, Medieval, and Renaissance Music.* Vol. 1 of *Historical Anthology of Music.* 2 vols. Rev. ed. Cambridge, Mass.: Harvard University Press, 1962.

Forkel, *Geschichte der Musik*

Forkel, Johann N. *Allgemeine Geschichte der Musik.* 2 vols. Leipzig: Im Schwickertschen Verlage, 1788–1801.

Funck, *Deutsche Lieder*

Funck, Heinz, ed. *Deutsche Lieder des 15. Jahrhunderts aus fremden Quellen zu 3 und 4 Stimmen.* Vol. 45 of *Das Chorwerk.* Edited by Friedrich Blume. 99 vols. Wolfenbüttel: Möseler Verlag, 1929–63.

Gaines, *Rhau: Tricinia*

Gaines, Charles T. "Georg Rhau: Tricinia, 1542." Ph.D. diss., Union Theological Seminary, 1970.

Geering-Trümpy, *Liederbuch des Heer*

Geering, Arnold, and Hans Trümpy, eds. *Das Liederbuch des Johannes Heer von Glarus: Ein Musikheft aus der Zeit des Humanismus (Codex 462 der Stiftsbibliothek St. Gallen).* Basel: Bärenreiter Verlag, 1967.

Gérold, *Manuscrit de Bayeux*

Gérold, Théodore. *Le Manuscrit de Bayeux: text et musique d'un recueil de chansons du XVe siècle.* Strasbourg: Librairie Istra, 1921.

Ghiselin: *Johannes Ghiselin-Verbonnet: Opera om-*
Opera Omnia *nia.* Edited by Clytus Gottwald. 4 vols. [Rome]: American Institute of Musicology, 1961–68.

Ghizeghem: *Hayne van Ghizeghem: Opera omnia.*
Opera Omnia Edited by Barton Hudson. Vol. 74 of *Corpus mensurabilis musicae.* [Rome]: American Institute of Musicology, 1977.

Giesbert, *Ein* Giesbert, Franz J., ed. *Ein altes*
altes Spielbuch *Spielbuch aus der Zeit um 1500 mit 3, 4, und 5 Stimmen für Blockflöten oder beliebige andere Instrumente: Pergament-Handschrift (Liber Fridolini Sichery) der Stiftsbibliothek zu St. Gallen.* 2 vols. Mainz: B. Schott's Söhne, 1936.

Goldthwaite, Goldthwaite, Scott. "Rhythmic Pat-
Rhythmic terns and Formal Symmetry in the Fif-
Patterns and teenth Century Chanson." Ph.D.
Formal Sym- diss., Harvard University, 1955.
metry

Gombosi, Gombosi, Otto J. *Jacob Obrecht: Eine*
Obrecht *stilkritische Studie.* Leipzig: Breitkopf & Härtel, 1925.

Greenberg- Greenberg, Noah, and Paul Maynard.
Maynard, *An Anthology of Early Renaissance Mu-*
Anthology of *sic.* New York: W. W. Norton, 1975.
Early Renais-
sance Music

Hawkins, Hawkins, Sir John. *A General History of*
History of *the Science and Practice of Music.* 2 vols.
Music Reprint. New York: Dover Publications, 1963.

Hewitt, *Canti* Hewitt, Helen, ed. *Canti B. numero*
B. *cinquanta, Venice, 1502.* Chicago: University of Chicago Press, 1967.

Hewitt, Hewitt, Helen, ed. *Harmonice musices*
Odhecaton *Odhecaton A,* with edition of the literary texts by Isabel Pope. Cambridge, Mass.: The Mediaeval Academy of America, 1942.

Isaac: *Heinrich Issac: Weltliche Werke.* Edited
Weltliche by Johannes Wolf. Vol. 28 of *Denkmä-*
Werke *ler der Tonkunst in Österreich.* Vienna, 1907.

Jeffery, *Chan-* Jeffery, Brian. *Chanson Verse of the*
son Verse *Early Renaissance.* London: Author, 1971.

Josquin: Josquin des Pres. *Werken van Josquin*
Missen/ *des Pres: Missen; Wereldlijke Werken.*
Josquin: Edited by Albert Smijers (new eds. M.
Wereldlijke Antonowycz and W. Elders), ser. 4,
Werken vols. 2, 4, and 5. Amsterdam: G. Alsbach, 1924——.

Maldeghem, Maldeghem, Robert-Julien van, ed.
Trésor musical *Trésor musical: Collection authentique de musique sacrée et profane des anciens maîtres belges.* 29 vols. Brussels: C. Muquardt, 1865–93.

Maniates, Maniates, Maria R. "Mannerist Com-
Mannerist position in Franco-Flemish Polyph-
Composition ony." *The Musical Quarterly* 52 (1966): 17–36.

Merritt, Merritt, A. Tillman, "A Chanson Se-
Chanson Se- quence by Févin." In *Essays on Music*
quence by *in Honor of Archibald Thompson Davison*
Févin *by His Associates.* Cambridge, Mass.: Department of Music, Harvard University, 1957.

Marix, *Les* Marix, Jeanne. *Les musiciens de la cour*
Musiciens de *de Bourgogne au XVe siècle (1420-1467).*
la cour de Paris: Louise B.-M. Dyer, 1937.
Bourgogne

Miller, *Heinrich Glarean, Dodecachordon.*
Heinrich Gla- Edited by Clement A. Miller. 2 vols.
rean, Dodeca-* [Rome]: American Institute of Musi-
chordon cology, 1965.

Newton, Newton, Paul G. "Florence, Bib-
Florence 2439 lioteca del Conservatorio di Musica Luigi Cherubini, Manuscript Basevi 2439." Ph.D. diss., North Texas State University, 1968.

Obrecht: Jacob Obrecht. *Werken van Jacob*
Missen/ *Obrecht: Missen; Motetten.* Edited by
Obrecht: Johannes Wolf. Reprint. Leipzig:
Motetten Breitkopf & Härtel, 1968.

Obrecht: *Jacobus Obrecht: Opera omnia.* Edited by
Missen (Smij- Albert Smijers. Vol. 1, Fasc. 3. Am-
jers) sterdam: G. Alsbach, 1954.

Osthoff, Osthoff, Helmuth. *Josquin Desprez.* 2
Josquin vols. Tutzing: Hans Schneider, 1965.

Paris- Paris, Gaston, and François-Auguste
Gevaert, Gevaert, eds. *Chansons du XVe siècle*
Chansons *publiées d'après le manuscrit de la Bibliothèque Nationale de Paris.* Paris: Librairie de Firmin-Didot, 1935.

Parrish-Ohl, Parrish, Carl, and John F. Ohl, eds.
Masterpieces *Masterpieces of Music before 1750.* New
of Music York: W. W. Norton, 1951.

Picker, *Chan-* Picker, Martin. "The Chanson Al-
son Albums of bums of Marguerite of Austria: Manu-
Marguerite scripts 228 and 11239 of the Bibliothèque Royale de Belgique, Brussels." Ph.D. diss., University of California, 1960.

Picker, *Chanson Albums of Marguerite of Austria*

Picker, Martin. *The Chanson Albums of Marguerite of Austria: MSS 228 and 11239 of the Bibliothèque Royale de Belgique, Brussels.* Berkeley and Los Angeles: University of California Press, 1965.

Pope and Kanazawa, *Montecassino 871*

Pope, Isabel, and Masakata Kanazawa, eds. *The Musical Manuscript Montecassino 871: A Neapolitan Repertory of Sacred and Secular Music of the Late Fifteenth Century.* Oxford: Oxford University Press, 1978.

Riemann, *Handbuch der Musikgeschichte*

Riemann, Hugo. *Das Zeitalter der Renaissance bis 1600.* Vol. 2, Part 1 of *Handbuch der Musikgeschichte.* 2 vols. Leipzig: Breitkopf & Härtel, 1920–23.

Rokseth, *Treize motets et un prélude*

Rokseth, Yvonne, ed. *Treize motets et un prélude pour orgue parus chez Pierre Attaingnant en 1531.* Paris: Librairie E. Droz, 1930.

Schering, *Geschichte der Musik in Beispielen*

Schering, Albert, ed. *Geschichte der Musik in Beispielen.* Leipzig: Breitkopf & Härtel, 1931.

Seay, *Thirty Chansons*

Seay, Albert, ed. *Thirty Chansons for Three and Four Voices from Attaingnant's Collections.* New Haven, Connecticut: Yale University Press, 1960.

Shipp, *Chansonnier of Dukes of Lorraine*

Shipp, Clifford M. "A Chansonnier of the Dukes of Lorraine: The Paris Manuscript 'fonds français 1597.' " Ph.D. diss., North Texas State University, 1960.

Smijers, *Van Ockeghem tot Sweelinck*

Smijers, Albert, ed. *Van Ockeghem tot Sweelinck,* 7 vols. Amsterdam: G. Alsbach, 1939–52.

Thompson, *Appenzeller*

Thompson, Glenda G. "Benedictus Appenzeller: *Maître de la chapelle* to Mary of Hungary and *Chansonnier.*" Ph.D. diss., University of North Carolina, 1975.

Whisler, *Munich 1516*

Whisler, Bruce A. "Munich, *Mus. MS. 1516:* A Critical Edition." Ph.D. diss., University of Rochester, 1974.

Wolf, *Music of Earlier Times*

Wolf, Johannes, ed. *Music of Earlier Times (13th Century to Bach), Vocal & Instrumental Examples.* New York: Broude Brothers, 1946.

Wolf, *Oud-Nederlandsche Liederen*

Wolf, Johannes, ed. *25 driestemmige Oud-Nederlandsche Liederen uit het Einde der viftiende Eeuw naar den Codex London British Museum Additional MSS. 35087.* Amsterdam: G. Alsbach and Leipzig: Breitkopf & Härtel, 1910.

Wolff, *Casanatense 2856*

Wolff, Arthur S. "The Chansonnier Biblioteca Casanatense 2856, Its History, Purpose, and Music." Ph.D. diss., North Texas State University, 1970.

Appendix B: Contents of London Add. 35087

A complete list of the seventy-eight compositions from London Add. 35087 is given below in the order in which the pieces appear in the manuscript. Although the accompanying data for the fifty-four French, Flemish, Latin, and Italian compositions not contained in this anthology exclude text sources and related compositions, the partial lists of concordances may be useful to the reader. Partial texts, such as a single stanza of a free chanson or a chanson refrain, are underlaid in these works except where otherwise noted. The titles of the twenty-four chansons of this edition are marked by asterisks to establish the positions of the pieces within the source. See Appendix A: Sources for bibliographic details and expansion of *sigla* used below. Composer-names are given in the form in which they appear in the various sources.

1. *O vos omnes*

[Loyset Compère/Jacobus Obrecht]; 3 voices; fols. 1ᵛ–2; the first fifteen notes of the T are also found on fol. 1.

MANUSCRIPTS

Bologna Q 17, fol. 11ᵛ; Loyset Compere; *a 3*; text in CT and incipit "O vos omnes" in S and T.

Bologna Q 18, fol. 65ᵛ; anon.; *a 3*; incipit "Tant hai dennuy" in all voices.

Brussels IV.90–Tournai 94, no. 7; anon.; S and T only, with text.

Brussels 228, fol. 59ᵛ; anon.; *a 3*; text "O devotz cueurs" in S and T, and text "O vos omnes" in B.

Copenhagen 1848, p. 117; anon.; *a 3*; texts "Tant ay dennuy" in S and "Tant ay dennuy O vos omnes" in CT.

Florence 107ᵇⁱˢ, fol. 35ᵛ; anon.; *a 3*; incipit "O vos omnes" in S.

Paris 1597, fol. 28ᵛ; anon.; *a 3*; text "Tant ay dennuyt" in S and T.

St. Gall 463, no. 19; Jacobus Obrecht; S only, with text.

EARLY PRINTED COLLECTION

Rhaw 1542⁸, no. 15; Loyset Compere; *a 3*; text in all voices.

MODERN EDITIONS

Besseler, *Die Musik des Mittelalters und der Renais-* sance, p. 231; Loyset Compère (after Obrecht: *Motetten*).

Compère: *Opera Omnia*, 5:4; text "O devotz cueurs" in S and T, and text "O vos omnes" in CT (after Brussels 228).

Davison-Apel, *Historical Anthology of Music*, 1:80; Jacob Obrecht (after Obrecht: *Motetten*).

Gaines, *Rhau: Tricinia*, no. 15; Loyset Compère (after Rhaw 1542⁸).

Maldeghem, *Trésor musical*, 23 (1887): 23; anon. (after Brussels 228).

Obrecht: *Motetten*, 6:173; (after Florence 107ᵇⁱˢ).

Picker, *Chanson Albums of Marguerite*, 2:271; Loyset Compère (after Brussels 228).

Picker, *Chanson Albums of Marguerite of Austria*, p. 391; Loyset Compère (after Brussels 228).

Schering, *Geschichte der Musik in Beispielen*, p. 49; Jacob Obrecht (after Obrecht: *Motetten*).

Shipp, *Chansonnier of the Dukes of Lorraine*, p. 343; Compère (after Paris 1597).

INTABULATION

Brown, *Instrumental Music Printed before 1600*, lists 1531₇, fol. 108, no. 10.

2. *Erubescat Judeus infelix*

Anon.; 3 voices; fols. 2ᵛ–3.

3. *Miserere mihi Domine*

Anon.; 3 voices; fol. 3ᵛ; incomplete: T lacking.

4. *Parce Domine*

[Jacob Obrecht]; 3 voices; fol. 4; incomplete: S and CT lacking.

MANUSCRIPTS

Bologna Q 17, fol. 2; anon.; *a 3*; text in CT, and incipit "Parce domine populo tuo" in T; S lacking.

Brussels IV.90—Tournai 94, no. 6; anon.; S and T only, with text.

Cambridge 1760, fol. 46ᵛ; Obrek; *a 3*; text in all voices.

Copenhagen 1848, p. 99; anon.; *a 3*; incipit "Parce domine" in S and T.

St. Gall 463, no. 128; Jacobus Obrecht; S and A only, with text.

EARLY PRINTED COLLECTION

Glareanus 1547[1], p. 260; Jacob Obrecht; *a 3*; text "Parce Domine" in all voices.

MODERN EDITIONS

Forkel, *Geschichte der Musik,* 2:524; Jacob Obrecht (source not given).

Miller, *Heinrich Glarean, Dodecachordon,* 2:327; Jacob Obrecht (after Glareanus 1547[1]).

Parrish-Ohl, *Masterpieces of Music,* p. 56; Jacob Obrecht (after Glareanus 1547[1]).

Rokseth, *Treize motets et un prélude,* p. 24; Jacob Obrecht (after Glareanus 1547[1]).

INTABULATION

Brown, *Instrumental Music Printed before 1600,* lists 1531[7], fol. 117, no. 13.

*5. Du bon du cueur ma chiere dame

Anon.; 3 voices; fols. 4[v]–5.

6. Mijn morken gaf mij een jonch wijff

Anon.; 3 voices; fols. 5[v]–6.

MODERN EDITIONS

Funck, *Deutsche Lieder,* no. 13; anon. (after London Add. 35087).

Wolf, *Music of Earlier Times,* no. 16; anon. (after London Add. 35087).

Wolf, *Oud-Nederlandsche Liederen,* p. 1; anon. (after London Add. 35087).

7. Ic weet een molenarynne

Anon.; 3 voices; fols. 6[v]–7.

MODERN EDITIONS

Funck, *Deutsche Lieder,* no. 12; anon. (after London Add. 35087).

Wolf, *Oud-Nederlandsche Liederen,* p. 2; anon. (after London Add. 35087).

8. Quant je vous voye

[Josquin Desprez]; 3 voices; fols. 7[v]–9.

EARLY PRINTED COLLECTIONS

Antico 1536[1], fol. 14[v]; Josquin; *a 3*; text in all voices.

Rhaw 1542[8], no. 87; Josquin; *a 3*; text in all voices.

MODERN EDITIONS

Benthem, *Josquin's Three-part "Chansons rustiques,"* p. 435 (excerpts after London Add. 35087 and Antico 1536[1]).

Gaines, *Rhau: Tricinia,* no. 87; Josquin des Prez (after Rhaw 1542[8]).

Josquin: *Wereldlijke Werken,* ser. 4, vol. 5:40 (after London Add. 35087, Antico 1536[1], and Rhaw 1542[8]).

*9. Adieu m'amour du temps passé

Anon.; 3 voices; fols. 9[v]–10.

10. Tristis est anima mea

Anon.; 3 voices; fols. 10[v]–11.

11. Fortuna desperata

[Antoine Busnois]; 3 voices; fols. 11[v]–12.

MANUSCRIPTS

Florence 121, fol. 25[v]; anon.; *a 3*; incipit "Fortuna desperata" in all voices.

Paris 4379—Seville 5–I–43, fol. 40[v]; anon.; *a 4*; (with *si placet* voice); text in S and incipit "Fortuna desperata" in three lower voices.

Paris Vm[7] 676, fol. 24[v]; anon.; *a 4*; text in S and incipit "Fortuna desperata" in three lower voices.

Perugia 431, fol. 83[v]; anon.; *a 3*; incipit "Fortuna desperata" in S.

Perugia 431, fol. 84[v]; anon.; *a 4*; text in S.

St. Gall 462, fol. 6[v]; anon.; *a 4*; text in S and A.

St. Gall 463, no. 144; anon.; S and A only, with text.

Segovia, fol. 174; Anthonius Busnoys; *a 3*; text in S and incipit "fortuna disperata" in T and CT.

Zwickau 78.3, no. 54; anon.; *a 4.*

EARLY PRINTED COLLECTION

Petrucci 1504[3], fol. 126[v]; anon.; *a 4*; incipit "Fortuna desperata" in S and incipit "Fortuna" in three lower voices.

MODERN EDITIONS

Bernoulli, *Aus Liederbüchern der Humanistenzeit,* p. 36; anon. (after Paris 4379—Seville 5–I–43).

Isaac: *Weltliche Werke,* 28:190; anon. (after Paris 4379—Seville 5–I–43).

Josquin: *Missen,* 1:105; anon. (after London Add. 35087).

Josquin: *Missen,* 1:106; anon. (after Petrucci 1504[3]).

Josquin: *Wereldlijke Werken,* ser. 4, vol. 4:25; Busnoys (after London Add. 35087).

Obrecht: *Missen,* 1:136; anon. (after Paris 4379—Seville 5–I–43).

Obrecht: *Missen* (Smijers), 1:170; Busnoys (after London Add. 35087).

Rokseth, *Treize motets et un prélude,* p. 55; anon. (after London Add. 35087).

INTABULATIONS

Brown, *Instrumental Music Printed before 1600,* lists 1507[2], fol. 38[v], no. 29, and 1531[7], fol. 83[v], no. 2.

The following four-voice settings contain the three voices from London Add. 35087 with a dissimilar A in each: (1) Bologna Q 16, fol. 117[v]; anon.; *a 4*; incipit "Fortuna desperata" in all voices. (2) Florence 2439, fol. 22[v], anon.; *a 4*; text "Poi ch te hebi nel core" in S and incipit "Poi ch te hebi" in A. (3) London Add. 31922, fol. 4[v], anon.; *a 4*; incipit "Fortune esperee" in all voices.

12. En l'ombre d'ung buisonnet

[Josquin Desprez]; 3 voices; fols. 12ᵛ–13.

MANUSCRIPTS

Monophonic Version: Paris 9346, fol. 104ᵛ (published in Gérold, *Manuscrit de Bayeux*, no. 101).

Bologna Q 17, fol. 45ᵛ; Josquin; *a 3*; incipit "En lombre dung buisonet" in all voices.

Brussels IV.90—Tournai 94, no. 8; anon.; S and T only, with text.

EARLY PRINTED COLLECTIONS

Antico 1536¹, fol. 7ᵛ; Josquin; *a 3*; text in all voices.

Egenolff [c. 1535]¹⁴, III, no. 27; anon.; S only, with incipit "En lombre."

Scotto 1562⁹, p. 19; Josquin; *a 3*; text in all voices.

Le Roy and Ballard 1578¹⁵, fol. 9; Josquin; *a 3*; text in all voices.

MODERN EDITION

Josquin: *Wereldlijke Werken*, ser. 4, vol. 5:26 (after Bologna Q 17, London Add. 35087, Antico 1536¹, Egenolff [c. 1535]¹⁴, Scotto 1562⁹, and Le Roy and Ballard 1578¹⁵).

INTABULATION

Brown, *Instrumental Music Printed before 1600*, lists 1533₁, fol. 45, no. 35.

13. Duert derven van u, mijn lief, mijn her versteent

Anon.; 3 voices; fols. 13ᵛ–14.

MODERN EDITION

Wolf, *Oud-Nederlandsche Liederen*, p. 3; anon. (after London Add. 35087).

14. Mijns liefkins claer anscauwen

Anon.; 3 voices; fols. 14ᵛ–15.

MODERN EDITION

Wolf, *Oud-Nederlandsche Liederen*, p. 4; anon. (after London Add. 35087).

15. Ic truere ende ic ben van mynnen alzo sieck

Anon.; 3 voices; fols. 15ᵛ–16.

EARLY PRINTED COLLECTION

Rhaw 1542⁸, no. 64; anon.; *a 3*; text in all voices.

MODERN EDITIONS

Gaines, *Rhau: Tricinia*, no. 64; anon. (after Rhaw 1542⁸).

Wolf, *Oud-Nederlandsche Liederen*, p. 6; anon. (after London Add. 35087).

16. Pauper sum ego

[Josquin Desprez]; 3 voices; fols. 16ᵛ–17.

MANUSCRIPTS

Brussels 228, fols. 58ᵛ–59; anon.; *a 3*; text "Ce povre mendiant" in S and T and incipit "Pauper sum ego" in *baricanor*.

Florence 2439, fol. 89ᵛ; Josquin; *a 3*; incipit "Fortune destrange plummaige" in S and T and text "Pauper sum ego" in CT.

MODERN EDITIONS

Josquin: *Wereldlijke Werken*, ser. 4, vol. 4:22 (after Brussels 228, Florence 2439, and London Add. 35087).

Maldeghem, *Trésor musical*, 23 (1887): 21; anon. (after Brussels 228).

Newton, *Florence 2439*, 2:250; Josquin (after Florence 2439).

Osthoff, *Josquin*, 2:385 (after Brussels 228).

Picker, *Chanson Albums of Marguerite*, 2:268; Josquin des Prez (after Brussels 228).

Picker, *Chanson Albums of Marguerite of Austria*, p. 389; Josquin des Prez (after Brussels 228).

17. Peccantem me quotidie

Anon.; 3 voices; fols. 17ᵛ–19.

18. Mijns liefkins bruun ooghen

Anon.; 3 voices; fols. 19ᵛ–21.

MODERN EDITION

Wolf, *Oud-Nederlandsche Liederen*, p. 6; anon. (after London Add. 35087).

19. Mon mary m'a diffamée

[Josquin Desprez]; 3 voices; fols. 21ᵛ–22.

20. Ma maistresse, m'amye

Anon.; 3 voices; fols. 22ᵛ–23.

21. Helas! dame que j'ayme tant

Anon.; 3 voices; fols. 23ᵛ–24.

22. Si j'ayme mon amy

Anon.; 3 voices; fols. 24ᵛ–25.

23. Wan ic ghedincke der alderliefster mijn

Anon.; 3 voices; fols. 25ᵛ–26.

MODERN EDITION

Wolf, *Oud-Nederlandsche Liederen*, p. 8; anon. (after London Add. 35087).

24. Mij heeft een piperken dach ghestelt

Anon.; 3 voices; fols. 26ᵛ–27.

MODERN EDITION

Wolf, *Oud-Nederlandsche Liederen*, p. 9; anon. (after London Add. 35087).

25. Consummo la mia vita

[Johannes Prioris]; 3 voices; fols. 27ᵛ–28.

MANUSCRIPTS

Cambridge, 1760, fol. 86ᵛ; Prioris; *a 4*; (with *si placet* voice); text in all voices.

Florence 117, fol. 66ᵛ, anon.; *a 3;* incipit "Consumo la mia vita" in S and T.

Paris 1597, fol. 77ᵛ; anon.; *a 3;* incipit "Consumo la vita mea" in S.

St. Gall 462, fol. 48; anon.; *a 3;* incipit "Consomo" in all voices.

St. Gall 463, no. 170; anon.; S and A only, with incipit "Consumo la mia vita."

Washington, Laborde, fol. 136ᵛ; anon.; *a 4;* incipit "Consumo la vita mya" in all voices.

MODERN EDITIONS

Bukofzer, *Studies in Medieval and Renaissance Music,* p. 211; Prioris (after Cambridge 1760 and Washington, Laborde).

Rokseth, *Treize motets et un prélude,* p. 52; anon. (after Washington, Laborde).

Shipp, *Chansonnier of Dukes of Lorraine,* p. 560; Prioris (after Paris 1597).

INTABULATION

Brown, *Instrumental Music Printed before 1600,* lists 1531₇, fol. 115, no. 12.

26. Mon souvenir

[Hayne van Ghizeghem]; 3 voices; fols. 28ᵛ–29.

MANUSCRIPTS

Bologna Q 17, fol. 32ᵛ; Hayne; *a 3;* incipit "Mon souuenir" in all voices.

Copenhagen 1848, p. 122; anon.; *a 3;* text in S and incipit "Mon souuenir mi fait" in T and incipit "Mon souuenir" in CT.

Copenhagen 1848, p. 364; anon.; *a 3;* incipit "Mon souuenir my fait morir" in S and CT.

Copenhagen 1848, p. 450; anon.; *a 3;* text in S.

Florence 178, fol. 27ᵛ; Ayne; *a 3;* incipit "Mon souenir" in S.

Florence 2356, fol. 4ᵛ; anon.; *a 3;* incipit "Mon solvenir" in all voices.

London Royal 20 A XVI, fol. 27ᵛ; Heyne; *a 3;* text in all voices.

Paris 1597, fol. 26ᵛ; anon.; *a 3;* text in all voices.

Paris 2245, fol. 1ᵛ; Hayne; *a 3;* text in S and incipit "Mon souuenir my fait morir" in T and CT.

Rome 2856, fol. 124ᵛ; Haine; *a 3;* incipit "Mon souuenir" in all voices.

Rome C. G. XIII.27, fol. 52ᵛ; anon.; *a 3;* incipit "Mon souenir" in S.

Segovia, fol. 164; Scoen Heyne; *a 3;* incipit "Mon souuenir" in all voices.

Washington, Laborde, fol. 110ᵛ; anon.; *a 3;* text in S.

EARLY PRINTED COLLECTION

Petrucci 1501, fol. 90ᵛ; anon.; *a 3;* incipit "Mon souenir" in S.

MODERN EDITIONS

Birmingham, *Chansonnier of Duke of Orleans,* p. 76; Hayne (after Paris 2245).

Ghizeghem: *Opera Omnia,* p. 34 (after all of the above manuscripts and early printed collections).

Goldthwaite, *Rhythmic Patterns and Formal Symmetry,* p. 51; Hayne (after Paris 2245).

Gombosi, *Obrecht,* 2:5; Hayne van Ghizeghem (after Rome 2856).

Hewitt, *Odhecaton,* p. 394; Hayne (after Petrucci 1501).

Marix, *Les Musiciens de la cour de Bourgogne,* p. 120; Hayne (after Paris 2245).

Shipp, *Chansonnier of Dukes of Lorraine,* p. 336; Hayne (after Paris 1597).

Wolff, *Casanatense 2856,* 2:335; Haine (after Rome 2856).

INTABULATION

Brown, *Instrumental Music Printed before 1600,* lists 1507₁, fol. 35ᵛ, no. 21.

27. Mais que che fut secretement

[Pietrequin/Loyset Compère]; 3 voices; fols. 29ᵛ–30.

MANUSCRIPTS

Bologna Q 17, fol. 18ᵛ; Pierquin; *a 3;* incipit "Mes que che fu secretement" in all voices.

Copenhagen 1848, p. 130; anon.; *a 3;* text in S and incipit "Mais que ce fust secretement" in T and CT.

Florence 178, fol. 67ᵛ; Pietraquin; *a 3;* incipit "Meschin che fuis secretament" in S.

Florence 229, fol. 218ᵛ; anon.; *a 3;* text in all voices.

Rome 2856, fol. 140ᵛ; anon.; *a 3.*

Rome C. G. XIII.27, fol. 46ᵛ; Petrequin; *a 4* (with *si placet* voice); incipit "Donzella no men culpeys" in S.

Washington, Laborde, fol. 114ᵛ; anon.; S only, with incipit "Mais que ce fust secretement."

EARLY PRINTED COLLECTION

Petrucci 1501, fol. 93; Compere; *a 3;* incipit "Mais que ce fust" in S.

MODERN EDITIONS

Compère: *Opera Omnia,* 5:67 (after Petrucci 1501).

Hewitt, *Odhecaton,* p. 400; Compere (after Petrucci 1501).

Wolff, *Casanatense 2856,* 2:384; Compère (after 2856).

*28. N'est il point bien infortuné

Anon.; 3 voices; fols. 30ᵛ–31.

*29. Nostre saison est bien fortunée

Anon.; 3 voices; fols. 31ᵛ–32.

*30. Lessiez parler, lessiez dire

Anon.; 3 voices; fols. 32ᵛ–33.

31. Verlanghen, ghij doet mijnder herten pijn

Anon.; 3 voices; fols. 33ᵛ–34.

MODERN EDITION
Wolf, *Oud-Nederlandsche Liederen*, p. 10; anon. (after London Add. 35087).

32. Ut queant laxis

Anon.; 3 voices; fols. 34ᵛ–35; first line of text in S; incipits "Ut queant laxis resonare" in T and "Ut queant laxis" in CT.

33. Een boer, een boer so willic waghen

Anon.; 3 voices; fols. 35ᵛ–36.

MODERN EDITION
Wolf, *Oud-Nederlandsche Liederen*, p. 11; anon. (after London Add. 35087).

*34. Coment peult avoir joye

Jo. de Vyzeto; 4 voices; fols. 36ᵛ–37.

35. C'est mal sarchie vostre avantage

[Alexander] Agrico♭♮; 3 voices; fols. 37ᵛ–38.

MANUSCRIPTS
Copenhagen 1848, p. 225; anon.; *a 3*; text in S and incipit "Cest mal vostre avantage" in T and CT.
Florence 178, fol. 20ᵛ; Alexander; *a 3*; incipit "Id est trophis" in S.
Florence 229, fol. 65ᵛ; Alexander Agricola; *a 3*; incipit "Cest mal serche" in S and CT.
London Royal 20 A XVI, fol. 10ᵛ; anon.; *a 3*; text in S and incipits "Cest mal cherche" in T and "Cest mal" in CT.
Rome 2856, fol. 18ᵛ; Agricola; *a 3*; incipit "Cest mal chierce" in all voices.
Seville 5–I–43—Paris 4379, fol. 123ᵛ; Agricola; *a 3*; incipit "Cest mal cerchie vostre avantage" in all voices.
Verona, DCCLVII, fol. 26ᵛ; anon.; *a 3*.

EARLY PRINTED COLLECTION
Petrucci 1501, fol. 14ᵛ; Agricola; *a 4* (with *si placet* voice); incipit "Cest mal charche" in all voices.

MODERN EDITIONS
Agricola: *Opera Omnia*, 5:22 (after Petrucci 1501).
Boer, *Chansonvormen*, p. 63; Agricola (after Petrucci 1501).
Hewitt, *Odhecaton*, p. 244; Agricola (after Petrucci 1501).
Wolff, *Casanatense 2856*, 2:53; Agricola (after Rome 2856).

36. Verlanghen, ghij doet mijn herte pijn

Anon.; 3 voices; fols. 38ᵛ–39.

MODERN EDITION
Wolf, *Oud-Nederlandsche Liederen*, p. 12; anon. (after London Add. 35087).

37. Da pacem domine

[Alexander] Agrico♭♮; 3 voices; fols. 39ᵛ–40.

MANUSCRIPTS
Copenhagen 1848, p. 365; anon.; *a 3*; incipit "da pacem domine" in all voices.
Copenhagen 1848, p. 435; anon.; *a 3*.
Paris 1597, fol. 3ᵛ; anon.; *a 3*; text in all voices.

MODERN EDITIONS
Agricola: *Opera Omnia*, 4:47 (after Paris 1597).
Shipp, *Chansonnier of Dukes of Lorraine*, p. 248; Agricola (after Paris 1597).

38. Die crudekins die spruten

Anon.; 3 voices; fols. 40ᵛ–41.

MODERN EDITION
Wolf, *Oud-Nederlandsche Liederen*, p. 12; anon. (after London Add. 35087).

39. Waer is hij nu, die mij mijn hertekin doet dolen?

Laurentius d. a.; 3 voices; fols. 41ᵛ-42.

MODERN EDITION
Wolf, *Oud-Nederlandsche Liederen*, p. 14; anon. (after London Add. 35087).

*40. Qui est celuy qui dira mal du con

Anon.; 3 voices; fols. 42ᵛ–43.

41. Je voy, je viens

Anon.; 3 voices; fols. 43ᵛ–44.

MANUSCRIPTS
Copenhagen 1848, p. 169; anon.; *a 3*; text in S.
St. Gall 463, no. 44; anon.; S only, with text.

EARLY PRINTED COLLECTION
Antico 1520⁶, no. 5; anon.; S and B with text; T lacking.

MODERN EDITIONS
Adams, *Aspects of the Chanson*, p. 230; anon. (after London Add. 35087).
Brown, *Theatrical Chansons*, p. 126; anon. (after London Add. 35087 and Antico 1520⁶).

*42. J'ayme bien mon amy

[Johannes Ghiselin] Verbonnet; 3 voices; fols. 44ᵛ–45.

43. Wy en sullen niet bedien

Anon.; 3 voices; fols. 45ᵛ–46.

MODERN EDITION
Wolf, *Oud-Nederlandsche Liederen*, p. 15; anon. (after London Add. 35087).

44. Ic ben zo nau bedwonghen

Anon.; 3 voices; fols. 46ᵛ–47.

MODERN EDITION
Wolf, *Oud-Nederlandsche Liederen*, p. 16; anon. (after London Add. 35087).

45. *Ghisternavent was ic maecht*
Anon.; 3 voices; fols. 47ᵛ–49.

MODERN EDITION
Wolf, *Oud-Nederlandsche Liederen*, p. 17; anon. (after London Add. 35087).

*46. *Tout plain d'ennuy et de desconfort*
[Benedictus Appenzeller]; 3 voices; fols. 49ᵛ–51.

47. *Eij laes, aij mij*
Anon.; 3 voices; fols. 51ᵛ–52.

MODERN EDITION
Wolf, *Oud-Nederlandsche Liederen*, p. 18; anon. (after London Add. 35087).

48. *T'meiskin was jonck*
[Japart/Jacobus Hobrecht/Isaac]; 3 voices; fols. 52ᵛ–53.

MANUSCRIPTS
Bologna Q 17, fol. 68ᵛ; anon.; *a 4* (with *si placet* voice); incipit "De tous in busc" in all voices.
Florence 107ᵇⁱˢ, fol. 4ᵛ; anon.; *a 4*; incipit "De tusch in busch" in S.
Florence 178, fol. 75ᵛ; Iapart; *a 4*; incipit "De tusche in busch" in S.
Florence 229, fol. 162ᵛ; anon.; *a 4*.
Segovia, fol. 103; Jacobus Hobrecht; *a 4*; incipit "Tmeiskin was jour" in S.

EARLY PRINTED COLLECTION
Petrucci 1501, fol. 29ᵛ; Isaac (Bologna copy); *a 4*; incipit "Tmeiskin" in all voices.

MODERN EDITIONS
Hewitt, *Odhecaton*, p. 277; anon. (after Petrucci 1501).
Isaac: *Weltliche Werke*, 28:109 (after London Add. 35087 with A from Petrucci 1501).
Wolf, *Oud-Nederlandsche Liederen*, p. 20; Henricus Isaac (after London Add. 35087).

49. *Adieu solas, tout plaisir*
[Antoine de Févin]; 3 voices; fols. 53ᵛ–54; second stanza of text is given below S.

MANUSCRIPTS
Cambridge 1760, fol. 63ᵛ; Anth. de Fevin; *a 3*; text in all voices.
Florence 117, fol. 14ᵛ; anon.; *a 3*; text in S.
London Harley 5242, fol. 20ᵛ; anon.; *a 3*; text in all voices.

MODERN EDITIONS
Brown, *Parisian Chanson*, p. 161; Antoine de Févin (after Cambridge 1760).
Clinkscale, *Févin*, p. 451 (after Cambridge 1760).

50. *O Venus, vrauwe wat dedic gheboren*
Anon.; 3 voices; fols. 54ᵛ–55.

MODERN EDITION
Wolf, *Oud-Nederlandsche Liederen*, p. 22; anon. (after London Add. 35087).

*51. *James n'aymeray mason: je suis trop belle*
Jo. [= Jean] Mouton; 3 voices; fols. 55ᵛ–56.

52. *Je le laray puisqu'il m'y bat*
[Jean Mouton]; 4 voices; fols. 56ᵛ–57; *signum* in S marks the entry of a canonic A at the fifth below.

MANUSCRIPTS
Monophonic Version: Paris 9346, fol. 67ᵛ (published in Gérold, *Manuscrit de Bayeux*, no. 66).
Florence 2442, fol. 85ᵛ; Mouton; *a 3*; text in three voices; B lacking.

MODERN EDITION
Brown, *Theatrical Chansons*, p. 109; Jean Mouton (after London Add. 35087).

53. *Troest mij, scoen lief*
Anon.; 3 voices; fols. 57ᵛ–59.

EARLY PRINTED COLLECTION
Rhaw 1542⁸, no. 63; anon.; *a 3*; text in all voices.

MODERN EDITIONS
Gaines, *Rhau: Tricinia*, no. 63; anon. (after Rhaw 1542⁸).
Wolf, *Oud-Nederlandsche Liederen*, p. 24; anon. (after London Add. 35087).

54. *Een sottecluytte wil ic ons singhen*
Anon.; 3 voices; fols. 59ᵛ–61.

MODERN EDITION
Wolf, *Oud-Nederlandsche Liederen*, p. 26; anon. (after London Add. 35087).

55. *Dulcis amica dei*
[Johannes Prioris]; 3 voices; fols. 61ᵛ–62.

MANUSCRIPTS
Cambridge 1760, fol. 2; Prioris; *a 3*; text in all voices.
Copenhagen 1848, p. 413; anon.; incipit "Dulcis amica dei" in all voices.
London Add. 31922, fol. 88ᵛ; anon.; *a 3*; incipit "Dulcis amica" in S.
Paris 2245, fol. 31ᵛ; anon.; *a 3*.
Washington, Laborde, fol. 139ᵛ; anon.; *a 3*.

EARLY PRINTED COLLECTION
Attaingnant 1540^2, fol. 4; anon.; *a 3*.

MODERN EDITIONS
Birmingham, *Chansonnier of Duke of Orleans*, p. 135; anon. (after Paris 2245 with A from Paris 1597).

Rokseth, *Treize motets et un prélude*, p. 15; anon. (after Washington, Laborde).

INTABULATIONS
Brown, *Instrumental Music Printed before 1600*, lists 1529$_3$, fol. 7^v, no. 6, and 1531$_7$, fol. 106^v, no. 9.

The following four-voice settings contain the three voices from London Add. 35087 with a dissimilar A in each: (1) Cambrai 125–128, fol. 133^v; anon.; *a 4*; text in all voices. (2) St. Gall 462, fol. 1; anon.; *a 4*; text in S and incipit "Dulcis amica dei" in T. St. Gall 463, no. 140; anon.; S and A only, with text. (3) Paris 1597, fol. 4^v, anon.; *a 4*; text in all voices.

56. Ric God, wie sal ic claghen

Anon.; 3 voices; fols. 62^v–64.

EARLY PRINTED COLLECTION
Rhaw 1542^8, no. 61; anon.; *a 3*; text in all voices.

MODERN EDITIONS
Gaines, *Rhau: Tricinia*, no. 61; anon. (after Rhaw 1542^8).

Wolf, *Oud-Nederlandsche Liederen*, p. 28; anon. (after London Add. 35087)

57. Ic weet een vraukin wel bereit

Anon.; 3 voices; fols. 64^v–66.

MODERN EDITION
Wolf, *Oud-Nederlandsche Liederen*, p. 30; anon. (after London Add. 35087).

58. Quant je vous voy parmy les rues

Anon.; 3 voices; fols. 66^v–68.

59. Que n'est il vray ma joye

Anon.; 3 voices; fols. 68^v–69.

60. Rijck God, nu moet ic trueren

Anon.; 3 voices; fols. 69^v–71.

MODERN EDITION
Wolf, *Oud-Nederlandsche Liederen*, p. 32; anon. (after London Add. 35087).

61. Sourdes regretz

[Loyset Compère]; 3 voices; fols. 71^v–73.

MANUSCRIPTS
Brussels IV.90—Tournai 94, no. 5; anon.; S and T only, with text.

Brussels 228, fol. 54^v; anon.; *a 3*; text in all voices.

Florence 117, fol. 37; anon.; T and CT with text; S lacking.

Florence 2439, fol. 51^v; Compere; *a 3*; text in S and incipit "Sourdes regretz" in T and CT.

MODERN EDITIONS
Maldeghem, *Trésor musical*, 23 (1887): 17; Louis Compère (after Brussels 228).

Newton, *Florence 2439*, 2:152; Compere (after Florence 2439).

Picker, *Chanson Albums of Marguerite*, 2:256; Loyset Compère (after Brussels 228).

Picker, *Chanson Albums of Marguerite of Austria*, p. 379; Loyset Compère (after Brussels 228).

62. Noch weet ic een ionc vraukin fijn

Anon.; 3 voices; fols. 73^v–75.

MODERN EDITION
Wolf, *Oud-Nederlandsche Liederen*, p. 34; anon. (after London Add. 35087).

63. Vivo ego dicit Dominus

Anon.; 3 voices; fols. 75^v–76.

64. Sancta Maria, piarum piissima

Anon.; 3 voices; fols. 76^v–78.

65. Buvons, ma comere, et nous ne buvons point!

Benedictus Appe[n]sc[h]elders; 3 voices; fols. 78^v–79.

66. Helas! pourquoy me sui ge mariée?

Anon.; 3 voices; fols. 79^v–80.

67. Fors seulement

Anon.; 3 voices; fols. 80^v–81; incomplete stanza in all voices.

EARLY PRINTED COLLECTIONS
Antico 1520^6, no. 19; anon.; S and B with text; T lacking.

Formschneider 1538^9, no. 46; anon.; *a 3*.

MODERN EDITIONS
Picker, *Chanson Albums of Marguerite*, 2:381; anon. (after London Add. 35087).

Picker, *Chanson Albums of Marguerite of Austria*, p. 477; anon. (after London Add. 35087).

INTABULATION
Brown, *Instrumental Music Printed before 1600*, lists 1538$_2$, fol. G1, no. 46.

See Helen Hewitt, "*Fors seulement* and the Cantus Firmus Technique of the Fifteenth Century" in *Essays in Musicology in Honor of Dragan Plamenac on His 70th Birthday* (Pittsburgh, University of Pittsburgh Press, 1969), p. 115, and Martin Picker, ed., *Fors seulement: Thirty Compositions for Three to Five Voices or Instruments from the Fifteenth and Sixteenth Centuries*, Recent Researches in the Music of the Middle Ages and Early Renaissance, vol. 14 (Madison: A-R Editions, 1981), p.

xx (p. 84 has a transcription of the London Add. 35087 setting), for discussions of this setting's relationship to other *Fors seulement* works.

*68. C'est donc par moy qu'ainsy suis fortunée?

[Ninot le Petit]; 3 voices; fols. 81ᵛ–83.

69. Salve mater salvatoris

[Jean Mouton]; 4 voices; fols. 83ᵛ–84; the direction "Canon Qui se exaltat humiliabitur" is given above CT; a *signum* in CT marks the entry of the canonic voice to form a mirror canon with CT.

MANUSCRIPTS

Florence II.I.232, fol. 153ᵛ; Io. Mouton; *a 4;* text in all voices.

St. Gall 463, no. 91; Joannes Mouton; S and A only, with text.

EARLY PRINTED COLLECTIONS

Antico 1520², no. 1; Jo. Mouton; *a 4;* text in all voices.

Glareanus 1547¹, p. 464; Jean Mouton; *a 4;* text in all voices.

MODERN EDITIONS

Hawkins, *History of Music,* p. 343; Johannes Mouton (after Glareanus 1547¹).

Miller, *Heinrich Glarean, Dodecachordon,* 2:538; Jean Mouton (after Glareanus 1547¹).

Riemann, *Handbuch der Musikgeschichte,* 2, pt. 1:252; Jean Mouton (after Glareanus 1547¹).

Schering, *Geschichte der Musik in Beispielen,* p. 65; Jean Mouton (after Glareanus 1547¹).

Smijers, *Van Ockeghem tot Sweelinck,* 7:207; Joannes Mouton (after *Motetti novi libro tertio,* Venice, A. Antico, 1520).

70. Vray dieu d'amour

[Antoine Brumel]; 3 voices; fols. 84ᵛ–86.

MANUSCRIPTS

Monophonic Versions: Paris 12744, fol. 6ᵛ (published in Paris-Gevaert, *Chansons,* no. 8) and Paris 12744, fol. 84ᵛ (in Paris-Gevaert, *Chansons,* no. 123).

Florence 107ᵇⁱˢ, fol. 47ᵛ; anon.; *a 3.*

Heilbronn X. 2, no. 18; anon.; B only, with incipit "Vray dieu damours."

London Harley 5242, fol. 1ᵛ, anon.; *a 3;* text in all voices.

St. Gall 461, no. 27; An. Brumel; *a 3;* incipit "Vray dieu damours" in S.

Ulm 237ᵃ⁻ᵈ, no. 42; anon.; *a 3;* incipits "Vra dieu damours" in S and T and "Vra dieu" in CT.

EARLY PRINTED COLLECTIONS

Egenolff [c. 1535]¹⁴, III, no. 49; anon.; S only, with incipit "Vray dieu damours."

Formschneider 1538⁹, no. 4; anon.

MODERN EDITIONS

Brumel: *Opera Omnia,* 6:104 (after St. Gall 461).

Chaillon, *Le Chansonnier de Françoise,* p. 23; anon. (after London Harley 5242).

Giesbert, *Ein altes Spielbuch,* 2:64; An. Brumel (after St. Gall 461).

INTABULATION

Brown, *Instrumental Music Printed before 1600,* lists 1538₂, fol. B1, no. 4.

71. Plaine d'ennuy / Anima mea liquefacta est

Loyset Compere; 3 voices; fols. 86ᵛ–87; text "Plaine dennuy" in S and T and text "Anima mea liquefacta est" in CT.

MANUSCRIPTS

Bologna Q 17, fol. 6ᵛ; Loyset Compere; *a 3;* incipit "Playne denuy" in S and T and incipit "Anima mea liquefacta est" in CT.

Brussels 228, fol. 55ᵛ; anon.; *a 3;* text "Plaine dennuy" in S and T and text "Anima mea liquefacta" in B.

Brussels 11239, fol. 27ᵛ; anon.; *a 3;* text "Plaine dennuyt" in S and T and text "Anima mea liquefacta est" in B.

Florence 2439, fol. 50ᵛ; Compere; *a 3;* text "Plaine denuy" in S and T and text "Anima mea liquefacta est" in CT.

MODERN EDITIONS

Blume, *Das Chorwerk,* 3:23; Pipelare; text "Sur tous regretz" in all voices (after Maldeghem, *Trésor musical*).

Maldeghem, *Trésor musical,* 13 (1887): 37; Pipelare (after Brussels 228).

Maniates, *Mannerist Composition,* p. 26; Compère (after London Add. 35087).

Newton, *Florence 2439,* 2:150; Loyset Compère (after Florence 2439).

Picker, *Chanson Albums of Marguerite,* 2:259; Loyset Compère (after Brussels 228 and 11239).

Picker, *Chanson Albums of Marguerite of Austria,* p. 381; Loyset Compère (after Brussels 228 and 11239).

*72. Petite camusette

[Antoine de Févin]; 3 voices; fols. 87ᵛ–88.

*73. Fuyés regretz, avant que l'on savance

Anthoine Fevin; 3 voices; fols. 88ᵛ–89.

*74. Amy, l'aurez vous donc, fortune

Anon.; 3 voices; fols. 89ᵛ–90.

*75. Je my soloye aller esbatre

Anon.; 3 voices; fols. 90ᵛ–91.

*76. Dieu gard de mal de deshonneur

[Jean Mouton]; 3 voices; fols. 91ᵛ–93.

77. *On a mal dit de mon amy*

[Antoine de Févin]; 3 voices; fols. 93ᵛ–94.

Manuscripts

Monophonic Versions: Paris 9346, fol. 75ᵛ (published in Gérold, *Manuscrit de Bayeux*, no. 74) and Paris 12744, fol. 46 (published in Paris-Gevaert, *Chansons*, no. 69).

Cambridge 1760, fol. 47ᵛ; Anth. de Fevin; *a 3;* text in all voices.

Florence 117, fol. 7ᵛ; anon.; *a 3;* text in all voices.

London Harley 5242, fol. 41ᵛ; anon.; *a 3;* text in all voices.

St. Gall 463, no. 43; anon.; S only, with text.

Ulm 237ᵃ⁻ᵈ, no. 37; anon.; *a 3;* incipit "On a mal dy de mon amy" in all voices.

Early Printed Collections

Antico 1520⁶, no. 29; anon.; S and B with text; T lacking.

Attaingnant 1529⁴, no. 26; anon.; *a 3;* text in all voices.

Le Roy and Ballard 1578¹⁵; fol. 11ᵛ; Févin; *a 3;* text in all voices.

Modern Editions

Clinkscale, *Févin*, p. 474 (after Cambridge 1760).

Merritt, *Chanson Sequence by Févin*, p. 98 (after Cambridge 1760).

Seay, *Thirty Chansons*, p. 7; A. Févin (after Attaingnant 1529⁴).

78. *Dicant nunc Judei*

Anon.; 3 voices; fols. 94ᵛ–95ᵛ; incomplete text in all voices; incomplete music in T.

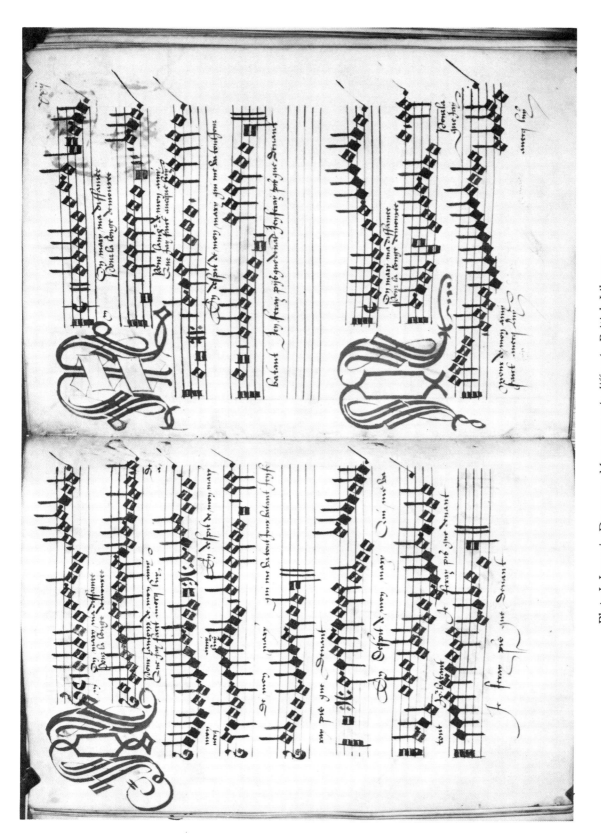

Plate I. Josquin Desprez, *Mon mary m'a diffamée*, British Library,
Manuscript Additional 35087, fols. 21v–22.
Actual size: 19.4 x 29.3 cm.
(Reproduced by permission of the British Library)

SELECTED CHANSONS

[1] Adieu m'amour du temps passé

[Anonymous]

Sans a-voir cau- se___ ne rai- son, Plus ne se-

- né, Sans a-voir cau- se ne_____ rai- son, Plus

- vez don- né, Sans a-voir cau- se ne_____ rai- son, Plus ne se- ray vos-tre mi-

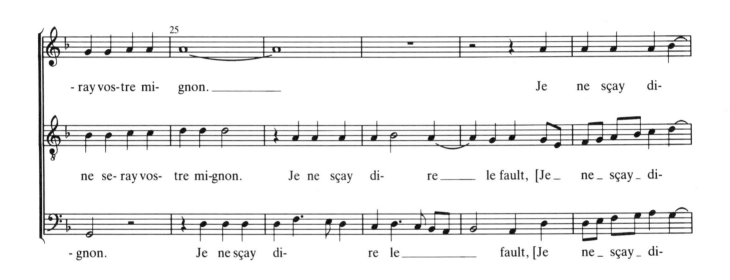

- ray vos-tre mi- gnon._____ Je ne sçay di-

ne se- ray vos- tre mi-gnon. Je ne sçay di- re_____ le fault, [Je_ ne_ sçay_ di-

- gnon. Je ne sçay di- re le_____ fault, [Je ne_ sçay_ di-

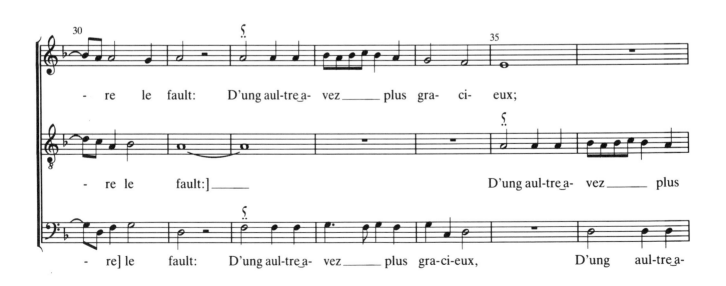

- re le fault: D'ung aul-tre a- vez_____ plus gra- ci- eux;

- re le fault:]_____ D'ung aul-tre a- vez_____ plus

- re] le fault: D'ung aul-tre a- vez_____ plus gra-ci-eux, D'ung aul-tre a-

Se le pre- nez,_____ il_____ ne m'en chault.

gra- ci- eux; Se le pre- nez,_____ il_____ ne_____m'en chault.

-vez plus gra- ci- eux; Se le pre- nez, il ne_____m'en chault.

Adieu m'amour du temps passé,	Goodbye my love of time past,
Car vous n'estez plus de saison.	You no longer love me.
Puisque congiet m'avez donné,	Since you left me,
Sans avoir cause ne raison,	Without cause or reason,
Plus ne seray vostre mignon.	No longer will I be your sweetheart.
Je ne sçay dire le fault:	I cannot say who is to blame:
D'ung aultre avez plus gracieux;	You have another more gracious;
Se le prenez, il ne m'en chault.	Go ahead, have him, I care not.

[2] Amy, l'aurez vous donc, fortune

[Anonymous]

6

Secunda pars *(from Uppsala 76a; S with text)*

Voy- [ez] en_____ moy vrays a- mours,___

[Voy- (ez) en_____ moy vrays_____ a-

- mours,] Quar dan- ger ne faut en so -

- las, Et rent je por- te ne_____

moins; _____ ____ De pas- ser ma_____ vie ne_____

fis, [ma_____ vie ne_____fis] onc- - ques las.

Amy, l'aurez vous donc, fortune,
Celle qu'ay choisy ma maistresse?
Temps est que v[ost]re rigueur cesse,
Car tousjours l'ay trouvé fortune.

Uppsala 76a
Voy[ez] en moy vrays amours,
Quar danger ne faut en solas,
Et rent je porte ne moins;
De passer ma vie ne fis oncques las.

Friend, will fortune then give you,
The one I have chosen as my mistress?
It is time that you not be so difficult,
For fortune has always been kind to me.

See in me true love,
For danger is not lacking in play,
And rank no less I have;
I've never spent my life unhappy.

[3] Buvons, ma comere, et nous ne buvons point!

Benedictus Appe[n]sc[h]elders

"Bu- vons,_ ma co- me- re, et nous____ ne

"Bu- vons, ma co- me- re, et nous ne

"Bu- vons, ma co- me- re, et nous ne

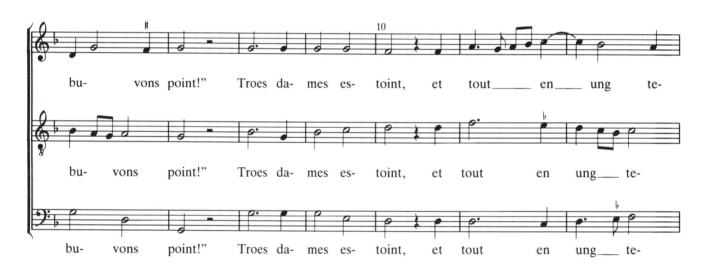

bu- vons point!" Troes da- mes es- toint, et tout____ en____ ung te-

bu- vons point!" Troes da- mes es- toint, et tout en ung____ te-

bu- vons point!" Troes da- mes es- toint, et tout en ung____ te-

- nant, Di- - sant, "ma co- me- re, nous ne bu-vons point." "Bu-

- nant, Di- sant, "ma co- me- re, nous____ ne bu- vons point."

- nant, Di- - sant, "ma co- me- re, nous ne bu-vons point."

vons, _ ma co- - me _ re, et nous ___ ne bu- vons point!"

"Bu- vons, ma co- me- re, et nous ne bu- vons point!"

"Bu- vons, ma co- me- re, et nous ne bu- vons point!"

"Buvons, ma comere, et nous ne buvons point!"
  Troes dames estoint, et tout en ung tenant,
  Disant, "ma comere, nous ne buvons point."
"Buvons, ma comere, et nous ne buvons point!"

Paris 9346
"Buvons, ma comere, etc.
  Il y vint ung rustre tout en beau pourpoint,
  Pour servir les dames tres bien et à point.
"Buvons, ma amie, etc.

"Buvons, ma amie, etc.
  Se dirent les dames: "Vecy bien à point;
  Faison bonne chere, ne nous faignons point."
"Buvons, ma amie, etc.

"Buvons, ma amie, etc.
  Le mignon commence, il ne tarda point.
  De servir s'avance tout à leur bon point.
"Buvons, ma amie, etc.

"Buvons, ma amie, etc.
  De chanter s'avance en doulx contrepoint,
  Et en grant plaisance vint fraper au point.
"Buvons, ma amie, etc.

"Buvons, ma comere, etc.
"Des maris doubtance nous n'en avons point.
  De eulx n'airons grevance, car ils n'y sont point."
"Buvons, ma comere, etc.

"Let's drink, friend, for we're not drinking!"
  Three women there were, in complete accord,
  Saying, "Friend, we're not drinking."
"Let's drink, friend, for we're not drinking!"

"Let's drink, friend, etc.
  There came a country-boy dressed in his doublet
  To serve the ladies well and he was so perfect.
"Let's drink, friend, etc.

"Let's drink, friend, etc.
  The ladies said to each other: "Now here's something!
  Let's live it up! Let's stop at nothing!"
"Let's drink, friend, etc.

"Let's drink, friend, etc.
  The dear boy begins; he did not tarry.
  He comes forth to serve them so very properly.
"Let's drink, friend, etc.

"Let's drink, friend, etc.
  He comes forth to sing in a sweet counterpoint,
  And with great delight clapped at the right moment.
"Let's drink, friend, etc.

"Let's drink, friend, etc.
"Of our husbands we don't have any fear.
  Nor will there be trouble, for they are not here!"
"Let's drink, friend, etc.

[4] C'est donc par moy qu'ainsy suis fortunée?

[Ninot le Petit]

C'est donc par moy qu'ainsy suis fortunée?
Infortuné, helas, suis sur ma foy!
Je suis infortunée!
Plus malheureux au monde ne cognois!
Aultre que moy n'est de tel heure née!

It is I then who alone am thus so fortunate?
It is I, alas, who am unfortunate! I swear!
I am unfortunate!
A more miserable man in the world I have never known!
No one but I has even been born under such a star!

[5] Coment peult avoir joye

Jo. de Vyzeto

_____ ne _____ luy_sou- vient.] Au boys sur la

__ luy_sou- vient.] Au boys sur la ra-

sou- vient.]_____ Au boys sur la ra- mé- e

- vient._____ Au boys____ sur la ra- mé- e_____

ra- mé- e N'a point_____

- mé- e N'a point_____ tout son __

N'a point tout_____ son_____ de- sir,_____ [son

N'a____ point tout son_____ de- sir,____ [de- - sir.]_____

__ tout son____ de- sir. De chan- ter il n'a

__ de- sir. De chan- ter il n'a cu-

de- - sir.] De chan- ter il n'a____ cu-

_____ De chan- ter il n'a____ cu- -

cu- re, _____ Qui vit ____ en des- - plai- sir.

- re, _____ Qui vit ____ en des- - plai- sir. _____

- re, _____ Qui _____ vit en des- plai- - sir.

- re, Qui vit en des- plai- - sir.

Coment peult avoir joye	How can one be happy
[Qui Fortune contrent?]	When fate has constrained him?
L'oysiau qui pert sa proye,	The bird which loses its prey
De neus ne luy souvient.	Does not think of us.
Au boys sur la ramée	In the woods on a branch
N'a point tout son desir.	He doesn't have all he wants.
De chanter il n'a cure,	He who lives in disfavor
Qui vit en desplaisir.	Is not inclined to sing.

[6] Dieu gard de mal de deshonneur

[Jean Mouton]

18

Dieu gard de mal de deshonneur
Celle que j'ay longtemps aymée.
[Je l' ay aymée de tout mon cueur,
Ma jeunesse est passée.]
Or voye je bien que c'est follie
D'y mettre ma pensée,
Car elle m'a dit en plorant
Nos amours sont finées.
Paris 9346
Despencer m'a faict mon argent,
A la maison d'ung tavernier,
Payer l'escot de maincte gent
Dont je n'en avoys pas mestier.
Chausses de verd m'a faict porter
Et souliers à poullaine,
Et par devant son huys passer
Mainctes foys la sepmaine.
Paris 1274
Je me suys mis à pourpenser
Quel desplaisir je luy ay faiz,
Mais mie g'ay peu aperceuz:
Ansy ne voudroy je l'aut[re] faiz.
De bien faire il en vient mesfaiz:
C'est verité prouvée!
Dieu soit loué de tout bienfaiz:
J'auré mieux l'aut[re]année.

Le verd je ne veux plus porter
Qui est piur est[at] aux amoureux,
Et de tout me veux exempter,
Celle ne me veult faire mieux.
De moy ne sera, semaindieux,
Dorenavans aymée,
S'il ne luy plaise, s'y aille ailleurs!
Elle est plainte et plorée.
Paris 12744
A pourpenser je me suis mys
Quel desplaisir luy avoys fait;
Jour de ma vie ne luy mesfis,
Ne ne le vouldroie avoir fait.
Pour bien faire souvent mal sourt,
C'est verité prouvée!
Dieu soit loué du temps qui court:
J'auré myeulx l'autre année.

Hellas! que vous a fait mon cueur?
Bien je le doy triste nommer.
Jamais ne veis ung tel malheur
D'homme pour loyaument amer;
J'en ay souffert maint douleur amer,
Mon oeil en rend larmes et plours;
Ainsy convient mon temps passer
Puisque j'ay perdu mes amours.

May God preserve from shame
The one I have loved for so long.
I loved her with all my heart.
My youth is gone.
Now I see it's foolish of me
To keep thinking of it,
For she told me crying
Our love is over.

She has made me spend my money
At the house of a tavern-keeper,
Buying rounds for many people
That I had no use for.
She made me wear green breeches
And crakows,
And pass before her door
Many times a week.

I began to think
How I displeased her,
But I found little:
I wouldn't have wanted to have acted in any other way.
Out of doing good a bad deed comes:
That's a proven fact!
May God be praised for all favors:
I'll have it better next year.

I no longer want to wear green,
Which is a worse state for lovers,
And I want to rid myself of all this:
She doesn't want to do better toward me.
By God, she will not by me
Henceforth be loved!
If it doesn't please her, let her go elsewhere!
She's been moaned and cried for [enough].

I have tried to think
How I could have displeased her;
I have never done anything to her,
Nor would I ever wanted to.
To do good, often one is deaf,
That's a proven fact!
May God be praised for the time that flies by:
I'll have it better next year.

Alas! what did my heart do to you?
I must call it sad, really.
Never have I ever seen such a misfortune
For a man that has so faithfully loved;
Because of it I have suffered so much bitter pain,
Because of it my eyes shed tears;
Thus I must spend my time
Since I have lost my love.

[7] Du bon du cueur ma chiere dame

[Anonymous]

Du bon du cueur ma chiere dame,
Vous supplie tres humblement
Que me rechevez doulcement
Pour vous servir de corps et d'ame,
Et je vous jure sur mon ame
Que vous serviray lealment.

From the goodness of my heart, my dear lady,
I beg of you very humbly
To keep me kindly in your service
To serve you body and soul,
And I swear to you on my soul
I will serve you faithfully.

[8] Fuyés regretz, avant que l'on s'avance

Anthoine Fevin

Fuyés regretz, avant que l'on s'avance
De vous bannyr, car du tout je vous quitte,
Et qui plus est, tout vous faiz, je despite,
Puisque mon deul s'est tourné en plaisance.

Flee, regrets, before one comes forward
To banish you, for I have left you for sure,
And what is more, everything you do I despise,
Since my suffering has turned to delight.

[9] Helas! dame que j'ayme tant

[Anonymous]

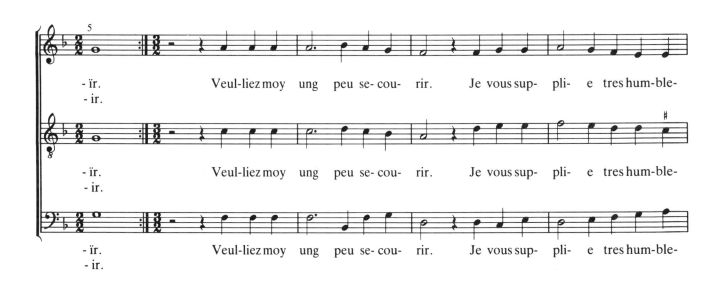

Helas! dame que j'ayme tant,
Plaise vous ma requeste ouïr.
Vous sçavez qu'il y a long temps,
Que j'ay desir de vous jouir.
Veulliez moy ung peu secourir.
Je vous supplie tres humblement,
Ou, du brief, m'y fauldra morir
En deul, en peine, et en tourment.

Alas! my lady that I love so,
May it please you to hear my request.
You know it has been a long time,
That I have desired to have you.
Please come to my aid a little.
I beg you very humbly,
Or shortly, I'll have to die
In pain, in anguish, and in torment.

Jeffery, *Chanson Verse*

Ne suis je pas bien maleureux,
Du monde le plus fortuné,
D'estre de vous si amoureux
Puis que de moy n'avez pitié?
J'ay le cueur de dueil sy oultré
Que tantost my fauldra mourir
Ou estre en la terre bouté
Si ne vous plaist moy secourir.

Am I not most unhappy,
The most fortunate man in the world,
To be so in love with you
Since you have no pity for me?
My heart is so overwhelmed with pain
That soon it will have to die
Or be thrown into the ground
Unless it pleases you to come to my aid.

El a la face si gentille
Et le corps fait à l'avenant,
Les tetins rons comme une bille,
Au monde n'est rien plus plaisant.
S'aupres d'elle estoye gesant
Mon cueur en seroit resjouy.
Je pris à Dieu le roy puissant
Que une fois j'en puisse jouyr.

She has such a sweet face
And a body so becoming,
Breasts like billiard balls,
Nothing in this world more pleasing.
If near her I were lying,
My heart would greatly rejoice.
I pray God, Almighty King,
That I can enjoy her one time.

Or me dictes, ma chere dame,
Qui estes plaine de si faulx tours;
Vous avez le cueur bien infame,
Je l'apersoy bien tous les jours.
Monstré m'avez signe d'amours
Et puis m'avez habandonné.
Mais vous verrez bien en briefz jours
Que mon cueur est ailleurs donné.

So tell me, my dear lady,
Who is so full of wicked tricks;
You are indeed quite heartless,
I notice it every day.
You did show me signs of love
Before you abandoned me.
But you will see very shortly
That my heart I have given to another.

[10] Helas! pourquoy me sui ge mariée?

[Anonymous]

Helas! pourquoy me sui ge mariée?
Vrais amoureux, ayes de moy pité,
Car, par ma foy, je suis desia lassée!

Alas! why did I get married?
True lovers, have pity on me,
For, indeed, I am already tired of it!

[11] James n'aymeray mason: je suis trop belle

Jo. [= Jean] Mouton

Ja- mes n'ay- me- ray ma- son: je suis trop bel- le;
Mon ma- ry est plus bel- lin qu'a-gneau qui bel- le:

Ja- mes n'ay- me- ray ma- son:_____ je suis trop bel- le;
Mon ma- ry est plus bel- lin_____ qu'a-gneau qui bel- le:

Ja- mes n'ay- me- ray ma- son: je suis trop bel- le;
Mon ma- ry est plus bel- lin qu'a-gneau qui bel- le:

Car il a bar-bouil- lé mon con de sa trou- el- le. Tou- te la nuyt, il
Il ne se-roit trou- ver mon con si n'a chan- del- le.

Car il a bar- bouil- lé mon con de sa trou- el- le. Tou- te la nuyt, il
Il ne se-roit trou- ver mon con si n'a chan-del- le.

Car il a bar-bouil- lé mon con de sa trou- el- le. Tou- te la nuyt, il
Il ne se-roit trou- ver mon con si n'a chan-del- le.

my di- soit que ma che-mi- se Luy nuy- soyt. Je la prins et la ge-

my di- soit que ma che-mi- se Luy nuy- soyt. Je la prins et la ge- sis

my di- soit que ma che-mi- se Luy nuy- soyt. Je la prins et la ge- sis

-sis en la ru- el- le, Mais en-co-re de- man-doit il de la chan- del- le.

en la ru- el- le, Mais en-co-re de- man-doit il de la chan-del- le.

en la ru- el- le, Mais en-co-re de- man-doit il de la chan-del- le.

James n'aymeray mason: je suis trop belle;
Car il a barbouillé mon con de sa trouelle.
Mon mary est plus bellin qu'agneau qui belle:
Il ne seroit trouver mon con si n'a chandelle.
Toute la nuyt, il my disoit que ma chemise
Luy nuysoyt. Je la prins et la gesis en la ruelle,
Mais encore demandoit il de la chandelle.

Never will I love a mason: I'm too beautiful;
For he has smeared my cunt with his trowel.
My husband is more of a ram than a lamb bleating:
He couldn't find my cunt even with a candle.
All night, he kept telling me that my smock
Was hindering him. I took it and threw it next to the bed,
And still, he kept asking for a candle.

[12] J'ayme bien mon amy

[Johannes Ghiselin] Verbonnet

J'ayme bien mon amy
De vrais amour certaine,
Car je sçay bien qu'il m'aime.
Et oussy, fai ge luy!

Lotrian 1543

Et puisqu'il est ainsi,
Que je congnois qu'il m'ayme,
Je seroys bien villaine
D'aymer aultre que luy.

Il n'est aultre plaisir,
En ceste vie mondaine,
Que d'aymer bien sans faindre,
Mais qu'on ayt bien choisy.

Madame, je vous pry
Que vous tenez certaine,
Que je prendray grand peine
Tousjours à vous obeyr.

I love my friend well
With a firm, true love,
For I know he loves me.
And I love him too!

And since it is so,
That I know he loves me,
I'd be naughty
To love anyone but him.

There's no other pleasure,
In this worldly life,
But to love without pretense,
Provided one has chosen wisely.

My lady, I beg you
To feel certain
That I'll take great pain
At all times to obey you.

[13] Je my soloye aller esbatre

[Anonymous]

Je my so- loy- -e al- ler _____ es- ba- - -

- tre A- vecq ches gen- [ti]lz ga- lans, [ga-

- - lans.] Mais main-te- nant je suis en la-

Je my so- loy- -e al- ler _____

_ es- ba- tre A- vecq [ches

gen- tilz ga- lans.] Mais main-te- nant _____ je suis _____

Je my so- loy- -e al- ler es- ba- - -tre, [al-

-ler es- ba- tre] A- - vecq _____ [ches _____ gen- tilz _____

_ ga- lans. _____ Mais main-te- nant je suis en

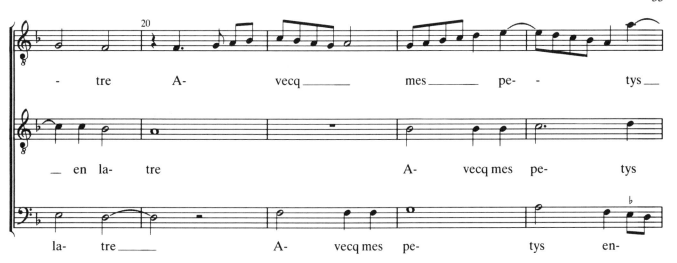

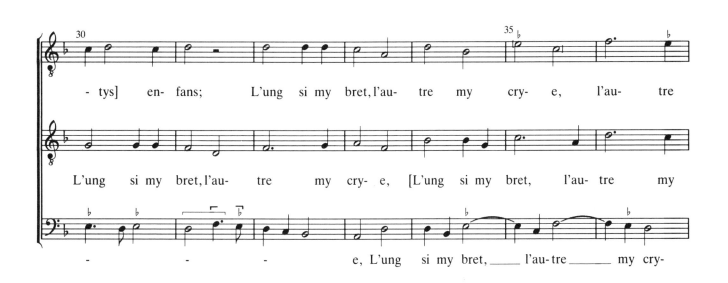

34

Je my soloye aller esbatre
Avecq ches gen[ti]lz galans.
Mais maintenant je suis en latre
Avecq mes petys enfans;
L'ung si my bret, l'autre my crye.
Dieu les benysse!

I used to go have fun
With these smooth-talking fellows.
But now I'm rich
With little kids;
One cries and the other so bellows.
May God bless them!

[14] Lessiez parler, lessiez dire

[Anonymous]

Lessiez parler, lessiez dire,
Lessiez parler qui voudra!
Au despit de jalosie,
J'aymeray qui m'aimera,
Et j'aymeray qui m'aimera!

Let them talk! let them chatter!
Let them talk who may wish to!
In spite of their jealousy,
I will love the one who will love me,
And I shall love the one who will love me!

[15] Ma maistresse, m'amye

[Anonymous]

Ma maistresse, m'amye,
N'oubliez point celuy
Qui point ne vous oublie!

My mistress, my beloved,
Don't forget the one
Who doesn't forget you!

[16] Mon mary m'a diffamée

[Josquin Desprez]

Mon mary m'a diffamée,
Pour l'amour de mon amy,
Pour la longe demourée,
Que j'ay faict avecque luy.
En despit de mon mary,
Qui me va tout jour batant,
Je feray pis que devant

Paris 12744

Aucunes gens m'ont blasmée
Disant que j'ay fait amy.
La chose tres fort m'agrée,
Mon tres gracieulx soucy.
Hé! mon amy!
En despit de mon mary
Que ne vault pas ung grant blanc,
Je feray pis que devant!

My husband has shamed me
Because of my lover,
Because of my long stay
That I had with him.
In spite of my husband,
Who beats me up all the time,
I'll even do worse than before!

Some people have blamed me,
Saying that I've taken on a friend.
The whole thing pleases me a lot.
It's my very pleasant worry.
Oh! my love!
In spite of my husband,
Who's not worth a big penny,
I'll even do worse than before!

Quant je suis la nuyt couchée
Entre les braz mon amy,
Je deviens presque pasmée
Du plaisir que prens en luy.
Hé! mon amy!
Pleust à Dieu que mon mary
Je ne veisse de trente ans!
Nous nous donrrions du bon temps!

"Sy m'amye est courroucée,
Pensez que j'en suis marry;
Car elle est sy mal traictée
Pour l'amour de son amy."
"Hé! mon amy!
En despit de mon mary
Qui ne m'ayme tant ne quant,
Je feray pis que devant!"

Si je pers ma renommée
Pour l'amour de mon amy,
Point n'en doy estre blasmée,
Car il est coincte et joly.
Hé! mon amy!
Je n'ay bon jour ne demy
Avec ce mary meschant:
Je feray pis que devant!

Lotrian 1543
Jeffery, *Chanson Verse*

Quand j'estoye couchée,
Entre les bras de mon amy
Je n'estoye pas fachée,
Comme je suis aujourd'huy.
O mon amy!
En despit de mon mary,
Qui me va tousjours batant,
J'en feray pis que devant!

J'esté mainte nuyctée,
Couchée avec mon amy,
Que l'on me cuidoit couchée,
En mon lict avecques mon mary!
O mon amy!
En despit de mon mary,
Qui me va tousjours batant,
J'en feray pis que devant!

When at night I'm in bed
In the arms of my lover,
I become almost limp
From the pleasure I get from him.
Oh! my love!
Would it please God that my husband
I would not see for thirty years!
Oh! we would have a good time!

"If my love is angry,
Imagine how sad I am;
For she is so mistreated
For the love of her lover."
"Oh! my love!
In spite of my husband,
Who doesn't love me not one whit,
I'll even do worse than before!"

If I lose my reputation
For the love of my lover,
I must not be blamed,
For he is trim and handsome.
Oh! my love!
Never do I have a good day or half a one
With this terrible husband:
I'll even do worse than before!

When I was in bed,
In the arms of my lover,
I was not as angry
As I am today.
Oh! my love!
In spite of my husband,
Who beats me up all the time,
I'll even do worse than before!

I have spent many a night
In bed with my love,
While they thought me in bed,
Sleeping with my husband!
Oh! my love!
In spite of my husband,
Who beats me up all the time,
I'll even do worse than before!

[17] N'est il point bien infortuné

[Anonymous]

42

à aul- truy a- ban- - - don- né?

_ a- ban- - don- né, a- ban- - - don- né?

- - don- né, _____ [a- ban- - - don- né?]

N'est il point bien infortuné,	Isn't he very unfortunate,
Qui de ceur ayme lealement,	Who has loved so faithfully,
Che que perpetuelement	Whose heart forever
Est à aultruy abandonné?	Is abandoned to another?

[18] Nostre saison est bien fortunée

[Anonymous]

A la froi-du- - re à la gel- lé- - - e.

A la froi-du- - re à la ___ gel- lé- - - - e.

A la froi-du- - re à ___ la gel- lé- - - e.

Nostre saison est bien fortunée,
Quant me parti de no maison
Pour aller couchier au buison
A la froidure à la gellée.

Our season is very fortunate,
When I tore myself away from our house
To go lie in the bushes
In the freezing cold.

[19] Petite camusette

[Antoine de Févin]

Pe- ti- te ca- mu- set- te, A la mort m'a-

Pe- ti- te ca- mu- set- te, A la mort

- ves mys, A la mort m'a- ves mys, [m'a-

m'a- - - - ves mys,_____ [m'a-

Pe- ti- te ca- mu- set- te, A

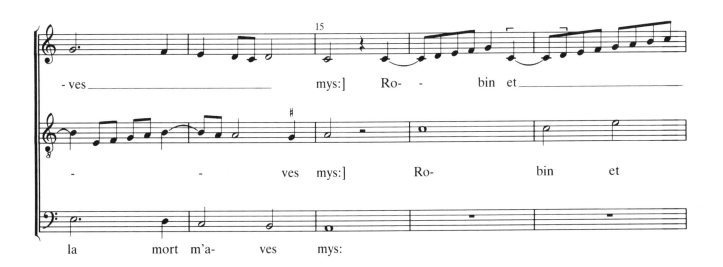

- ves_____ mys:] Ro- - bin et_____

- - ves mys:] Ro- bin et

la mort m'a- ves mys:

Petite camusette,
A la mort m'aves mys:
Robin et Marion,
Il s'en vont bras à bras,
Il s'en sont endormys.
Petite camusette,
A la mort m'aves mys!

My little snub-nose,
You have me close to death:
Robin and Marion,
They go about arm in arm,
They have fallen asleep.
My little snub-nose,
You have me close to death!

[20] Quant je vous voy parmy les rues

[Anonymous]

Quant je vous voy,

Quant je vous voy, [Quant je vous

Quant je vous

Quant je vous voy par- my les ru- -

voy] par- my les ru- - es,

voy par- my les ru- -

- es, Je vous sou- hai- de tou- te nu- e En- tre mes bras

Je vous sou- hai- de tou- te nu- e En- tre mes bras des- sus mon lyt,

- es, Je vous sou- hai- de tou- te nu- e En- tre mes bras des- sus mon lyt,

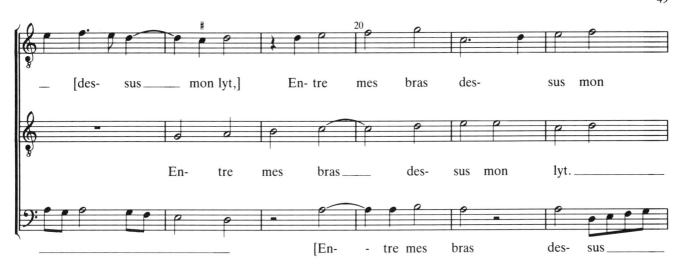

[des- sus ___ mon lyt,] En- tre mes bras des- sus mon

En- tre mes bras ___ des- sus mon lyt. ___

[En- - tre mes bras des- sus ___

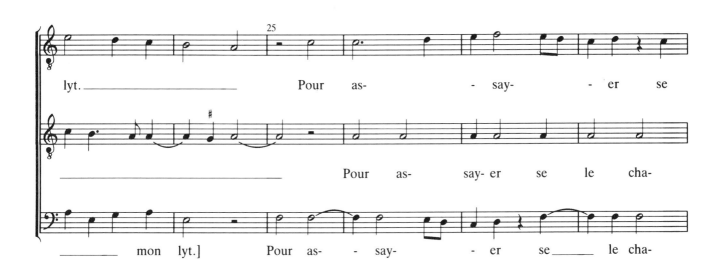

lyt. ___ Pour as- -say- - er se

Pour as- say- er se le cha-

___ mon lyt.] Pour as- say- - er se ___ le cha-

le cha- ly, ___ En- du- re bien ___

- ly, En- du- re bien, ___ En-

- ly, ___ En- du- re bien,

50

Quant je vous voy parmy les rues,
Je vous souhaide toute nue
Entre mes bras dessus mon lyt.
Pour assayer se le chaly,
Endure bien qu'on s'y reunie.

When I see you on the street,
My wish is to have you naked
In my arms and in my bed.
To try this out,
Please agree that we unite there.

[21] Que n'est il vray ma joye

[Anonymous]

Que n'est il vray ma joye,   Were my joy true,
Esperanche me fuisse.   Hope escapes me.

[22] Qui est celuy qui dira mal du con

[Anonymous]

Pour-tant   qu'à deux ge- noux,_____ on luy bail-   le   sa___   proy-   e.

___   Pour-   tant qu'à deux ge-   noux, on luy bail-   le   sa_____ proy-   e.

- tant   qu'à   deux____   ge- noux,   on   luy bail- le   sa   proy-   e.

Qui est celuy qui dira mal du con,
Celuy qui en dit mal, il n'est pas gentilhome!
Tout bien en vient, le solas et le joye,
Pourtant qu'à deux genoux, on luy baille sa proye.

Who will bad-mouth the cunt,
Who is doing so now, is not a gentleman!
All good pleasure and joy come from it,
Seeing that on one's knees, one gives it his spoils.

[23] Si j'ayme mon amy

[Anonymous]

Si j'ay- me mon a- my, Trop plus que mon ma- ry, En a- vez
Si j'ay- me mon a- my, Trop plus que mon ma- ry, En a- vez
Si j'ay- me mon a- my, Trop plus que mon ma- ry, En a- vez

vous mer- veil - le, [mer- veil- le?] Il n'est ou- vrier que
vous mer- veil- - le, mer- veil- le? Il n'est ou- vrier que
vous mer- veil- le, mer- veil- le? Il n'est ou- vrier que

luy, De che mes- tier jo- ly, Qui se faict sans chan- deil- - le!
luy, De che mes- tier jo- ly, Qui se faict sans chan- deil- - le!
luy, De che mes- tier jo- ly, Qui se faict sans chan- deil- - le!

Si j'ayme mon amy,
Trop plus que mon mary,
En avez vous merveille?
Il n'est ouvrier que luy,
De che mestier joly,
Qui se faict sans chandeille!

If I love my friend
Much more than my husband,
Are you astonished?
As a worker there's no one like him
In the marvellous job
That is done without a candle!

London Harley 5242

Mon amy est gaillard,
Et mon mari vieillart,
Et je suis jeune dame;
Mon cueur seroy paillart
D'aimer ung tel coquart
Veu qu'il est tant infame.

My friend is gallant,
And my husband an old man,
And I am a young lady;
My heart would be lecherous
To love such a cuckold,
Seeing he's so disgraceful.

Et quant j'ay mon mari,
Je n'ay point mon ami,
Ne chose qui me plaise;
Or fuyt enseveli
Et en terre pourri,
Si serois à mon aise!

When I have my husband,
And I don't have my friend,
Nothing pleases me;
Oh! if only he were buried
And rotting in the ground,
Would I be delighted!

Quant suys o mon amy,
Couché aupres de luy,
Il me tient embrassée.
Je n'ay aultre plaisir,
Aussi n'a il pas que luy,
Jamais n'en fuz lassée.

When I am with my friend,
Sleeping next to him,
He holds me in his arms.
I have no other pleasure,
Also he's the only one,
Never do I get tired of him.

Si j'ayme mon amy,
Qui est si tres gentil,
Ce n'est pas de merveille:
Car il n'y a que luy
Que mon cueur a choisi:
Nul à luy n'appareille.

If I love my friend,
Who is so gentle,
It is not astonishing:
For he's the only one
That my heart has chosen:
No one measures up to him.

Mon amy est gaillard,
Aultre en luy n'aura part,
Fors que moy, sur mon ame;
Car quant il me laissa,
Sa foy il me jura
Qu'il n'auroit aultre dame.

My friend is gallant,
No other will have a share,
Except me, I swear!
For when he left me,
He swore to me his fealty
That he would have no other.

L'on m'a donné se bruit
Que j'ayme mon amy,
Mais la raison est bonne:
Car tout le monde dit
Que je l'ay bien choisi
Pour ung tres honnestre homme.

The rumor about is circulating
That I love my friend,
And the reason is good:
For everyone says
That I have chosen well
For a very worthy man.

Responce:

Bien doibt etre marri,
Celuy qui est mari
D'une putain de feme,
Qui va veoir son amy,
Quant il est endormi:
Tant est orde et infame!

Il n'est poinct ung vieillart,
Mais trop sain et gaillard,
Que a pris tel coquarde,
Qui pour meme ung leard
Y cousta son coquart:
Aultre nul sa paillarde!

Response:

He has a right to be angry,
The one who is the husband
Of a harlot of a woman,
Who goes to see her friend,
When he is sleeping:
It's such filth and shamefulness!

He's not an old man,
Moreover, very healthy and gallant,
Who took on such a saucy,
She, who for very few pennies
Paid for her cocky:
There's no one more whorish than she!

[24] Tout plain d'ennuy et de desconfort

[Benedictus Appenzeller]

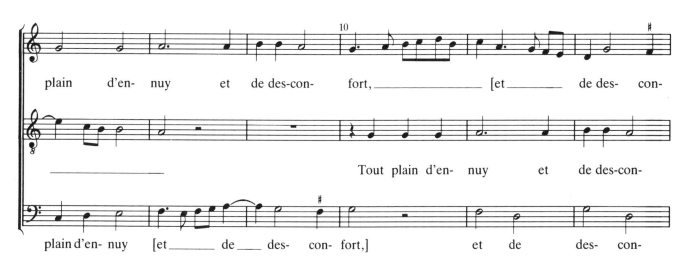

Tout plain d'ennuy et de desconfort,
Souvent je suis nul ne contredy
A mes doleurs que souvent je porte;
Seul regretant celle à qui trop fort
Ay mys mon ceur et aultres en oubly.

So full of grief and discouragement,
Often I don't find any answer
To the anguish I often bear;
Only regretting her in whom too strongly
I placed my heart and with that, forgot others.

DATE DUE

HIGHSMITH 45-220